Praise for Stephens G

"In *Jumbo,* Stephens Gerard Malone tak
well as deep into the recesses of the hum
tiniest woman and the world's largest elep novel
examines greed and cruelty, love and compassion, interspecies abuse and the tenacity of survivors. Moving, tender, and tough, Malone unwraps the Jumbo of myth and creates an unforgettable world. I loved this novel."

–BETH POWNING
bestselling author of *The Sea Captain's Wife*

"Malone's *Jumbo* takes us inside the greatest show on earth—our humanity and inhumanity—stripped to the bone. A book to hold tenderly."

–SHANDI MITCHELL
award-winning author of *Under This Unbroken Sky*

"*Jumbo* is an exquisitely crafted novel that takes readers deep into the intricacies of love, longing, and devotion. A thought-provoking novel you will absolutely want to read more than once."

–LAURA BEST
author of *Good Mothers Don't*

"Malone expertly weaves an interesting and realistic tale, shedding light on the eerie painted happiness of the circus world and the truths that lie beneath.... *Jumbo* is a tragic tale that balances beautiful storytelling with heavy themes. Malone skillfully transports readers to the captivating world of the 19th-century circus, where they will be enthralled by the story's realism and invested in the lives of its characters, leaving the book in the reader's mind long after the final page."

–ATLANTIC BOOKS TODAY

"Malone, like his character, is a master of cultivation, and [*The History of Rain*], like the gardens it imagines, is a wonder of patience and intricate attention. Wander through and try to take it all in. Everywhere you look, there is more than you expect."

–ALEXANDER MACLEOD
O. Henry Prize–winning author of *Animal Person*

"Transporting and profound, *The History of Rain* is a haunting tale of love, hope, truth, and beauty lost and found in unexpected places. This captivating novel had me turning pages late into the night."

–AMI MCKAY
bestselling author of *The Birth House*

"A spellbinding tale of enchantment, deception, and the impulses and illusions that make us human. Stephens Gerard Malone is a master, his writing a marvel of breathtaking tautness and force as he charts the darkness of war-ravaged Europe and the gilt, sun-drenched surfaces of Old Hollywood. A novel as dazzling as the gardens at the heart of it—astonishing."

–CAROL BRUNEAU
award-winning author of *Brighten the Corner Where You Are*

"Reader, let this beautifully crafted story transport you on a quest for love and belonging through war-ravaged Europe, the razzle dazzle of Old Hollywood, and the enchantment of grand landscape gardens. Evocative of both D. H. Lawrence and F. Scott Fitzgerald, Stephens Gerard Malone has created a sumptuous story of unrelenting tension, passion, and heartbreak."

–CHRISTY ANN CONLIN
author of *The Speed of Mercy* and *Watermark*

"*The History of Rain* is a moving and compassionate tale of war's devastation, the moral cost of survival, and one man's search for love. Writing with cinematic clarity, Stephens Gerard Malone proves again that he is a master of narrative tension and a first-rate historical novelist. This is a novel that leaves an indelible mark on the reader."

–IAN COLFORD
author of *A Dark House & Other Stories*

"Melancholic and spare, but not without hope, *The History of Rain* is a poignant work that says so much by leaving things unsaid….A love story you won't soon forget."

–[EDIT] MAGAZINE

JUMBO

JUMBO

STEPHENS GERARD MALONE

Vagrant
PRESS

Vagrant Press is an imprint of
Nimbus Publishing Limited
3660 Strawberry Hill St, Halifax, NS, B3K 5A9
(902) 455-4286 nimbus.ca

Nimbus Publishing is based in Kjipuktuk, Mi'kma'ki, the traditional territory of the Mi'kmaq People.

Printed and bound in Canada

Editor: Whitney Moran
Cover Design: Jenn Embree
Typesetting: Rudi Tusek
Jumbo image on p. 228 © iStock
NB1651

This is a work of fiction. While certain characters are inspired by real persons, and certain events by events which may have happened, the story is a work of the imagination not to be taken as a literal or documentary representation of its subject.

Library and Archives Canada Cataloguing in Publication
Title: Jumbo / Stephens Gerard Malone.
Names: Malone, Stephens Gerard, 1957- author.
Identifiers: Canadiana (print) 20230217222 | Canadiana (ebook) 20230217249
ISBN 9781774712030 (softcover) | ISBN 9781774712115 (EPUB)
Classification: LCC PS8626.A455 J86 2023 | DDC C813/.6—dc23

Nimbus Publishing acknowledges the financial support for its publishing activities from the Government of Canada, the Canada Council for the Arts, and from the Province of Nova Scotia. We are pleased to work in partnership with the Province of Nova Scotia to develop and promote our creative industries for the benefit of all Nova Scotians.

Based on true events.

jumbo: *19th c. originally of a person: origin unknown: popularized as the name of a zoo elephant sold in 1882*

OXFORD DICTIONARY

Bridgeport, Connecticut, 1891

She was once the most famous woman in the world, but never invited to his home in Bridgeport. Must be true then, talk of him dying. She thought he'd never die. So did he, probably. But here Nell was, and there it was—Marina, verandas and window awnings pooling in April heat, gulls hovering effortlessly over the distant sound, cherry blossoms raining on gardeners, open shirts dark with sweat, trimming lawns and filling carts with clippings of hedge as if nothing was about to change.

A cat by the door awkwardly licking its hind paw looked up, scurried from the approaching wheels. The silent men by her side made ready, but when helped from the carriage, one look told her: *Here's the cellar where washing and potatoes get delivered.*

"Good of you to come, Nell," greeted the woman in lavender, sounding as if the visit wasn't good at all, although the two Pinkerton men didn't give her much choice.

From the way Nancy Fish Barnum looked down her nose, Nell thought she'd stepped into something unpleasant getting out of the carriage, but decided if horseshit was on her shoes, too bad for the carpets.

"Wait here," Mrs. Barnum instructed the men.

Smelled of beer and onions. Not much for talking, but the younger fella said he'd brought his boy to Madison Square Garden once, lined up for hours on Broadway, back when everyone in the world wanted to see Nell and that elephant.

"You'll want to rest after your journey?"

"Rather get on if you don't mind."

Mrs. Barnum turned with a swoosh of skirts and disdain, meaning Nell was to follow her and that bloodstone at her throat, big as an apple. She wasn't wearing mourning one minute earlier than she had to.

But Nell didn't move. "Like I telegraphed you, Mrs. Barnum, I need to know we got an understanding."

The way those yards of satin and bows came crashing down like an angry wave hitting the beach. "Your benefactor is upstairs dying, and you dare go on about a pound of flesh like a—"

"Shylock? Yes, missus, reading Shakespeare is another trick I do, along with riding ponies through rings of fire. Now, we got a deal?"

Mrs. Barnum stopped dabbing her eyes, gave a twitch of the jaw. That'd do for an answer. Nell figured rightly the woman just wanted to get through this day and was angrily led past the kitchen where an old sort in a bandana, beet red from the heat, rolled pastry, didn't even look up. Nell'd seen spent horses the likes of her took out and shot, but cook kept on rolling.

Upstairs, drooping palms in Chinese ceramic lined a hall wide enough for two carriages to pass. Nell trotted to keep up. What was coming wouldn't be easy for the young wife, and Nell naturally wanted to feel sorry for Mrs. Barnum. Her being the second one—the first not even having letters carved on her marble. But here she was, looking like she feared catching whatever Nell had, terrified lest her hoity-toity neighbours see one of her husband's oddities come round. Something most folks paid good money for. What was it Barnum told her? Little Eyes Nell, you're the most famous person in America.

Used to be.

As far as Nell was concerned, if any of the good folks of Bridgeport be turning up their noses at anyone, it'd be at that wife of his. Marrying a man old enough to be her grandpa and everyone knowing why. But Marina would soon be hers—circus, too, without lacing herself into a tight corset for two shows a day, steaming under hot

Hippodrome lights. So, Nell gave Mrs. Barnum her due. But no pity, not for a woman who made Little Nell Kelly run to keep up.

"He mustn't be unsettled." Mrs. Barnum, hand on the doorknob. If the woman fretted why her man wished to spend his last moments with the likes of Nell, she kept it as tight as her laces.

The door shutting heavily behind her, a gloved hand masked medicinal air redolent of sandalwood and fish oil liniment. Bothered bits of dust swirled in beams slanting across walls papered in a dizzying pattern of greens. A mantel clock ticked, and tocked, the cold fireplace half circled by empty sofas. In wrought-iron birdcages hung by tall and wide windows, inmates under crepe coverings fluttered blindly at Nell's slow footsteps towards laboured breathing. There she found him, watched over by carved circus animals holding up the four-poster bed, shallow and sunken, a ridge of bones under sheets: what remained of the not-so-great-anymore man himself.

It gave her no pleasure, as she had hoped.

As Nell leaned closer, the sputtering of the ashen man's lungs grew troubled and faint, his mouth open, until he made no sound at all. She hadn't wanted to touch him, vowed she wouldn't, but watching him clutch at what precious few moments remained, Nell slipped her hand into his, remembering how bear-like and crushing it was to her as a child, how a pen in its grip once wielded the fortunes of men and animals, now bones and cold, but still pulsing. Her touch pulled him back from whatever gate he was looking through.

"You...Little Eyes?"

And for a moment, the great showman that Nell remembered. All glint and giggles. Not an old man she was happy to hasten to some powerful judgment. Death, an inconvenience he'd shrug off. Just you wait and see. Three rings, a matinee, and a nightly extravaganza. Still hawking the best seats, only twenty-five cents.

"Ladies and gentlemen, boys and girls, I give you...Little Eyes Nell."

Unexpectedly loud and forceful. Until the end. Her name barely a sigh.

"Missus says you gotta rest."

"What I'd give to hear Elephant Bill open the show, one more time."

Took both of hers to pull free of his icy hand. "Bill don't open the show anymore."

"What? What do you say?"

Guess Mr. Barnum forgot what happened to Elephant Bill. Nell didn't.

"Your missus…looks hopeful." She meant about him not dying.

He wheezed and plopped back onto his mountain of pillows. "Always were a good liar, Nell. One of the best. No, my dear, my time's come." Barnum patted his chest. "Or shall we say, it's come for my heart."

Stepping away, kind words of hope slipped out before she got the better of them. "The doctors?"

"If I'd known what a bunch of quacks they are, I'd have made them waddle around the ring a long time ago."

"Is there nothing?"

"No…no."

His eyes closed and his head nodded forward. Bloody hell if she'd come all this way just for him to die without knowing what he wanted. She gave him a shove.

"Huh? Nell? Yes…yes…you wear black. Not for me? I forbid it. Yellow's your colour, and I'm not gone yet. But you did wear black, once. I remember. For—"

"You don't got much time, Mr. Barnum."

Too true, he nodded. "Always had a hard streak to you, Nell. Even as a girl. You'd have made a wonderful showman. Left the circus to you if you were a man—well, a normal one."

Jibber jabber. Whatever he really wanted to say might take some time getting out. Him circling like he was, she hoped he had enough words left. Untying the ribbons to her bonnet, Nell carefully pulled it from her wig.

"What good's all this now, eh?" He weakly gestured, as if meaning Marina. "One day you'll know too; you'll be like me. But no man loved the Lord's mistakes more than Phineas Barnum." He began to cough. "That, I take proudly to my grave."

Nell poured him a glass of water and held it while he sipped.

"Thank you, my dear." Spittle rested on his lips. "I know you don't believe me, but you, Nell, you were my favourite."

"You forgetting about—"

"No. You promised, Nell, never to speak that name to me."

Ah, there he was, able to anger, still the old Prince of Humbugs, the Greatest-Show-on-Earth Barnum. Hard, mean stare, eyes knifing right through you, cold ugly smile. Always getting his way, figuring how to profit. She set the glass down, picked up the etching of a benign younger Barnum framed in silver, surrounded by children, an elephant under one arm, a pony under the other, while leading a menagerie from Madison Square Garden. How had she not seen this before? And damned if it wasn't clear to Nell right then why she'd been summoned.

"Not enough I kept my promise, now you want me to forget?"

"I'm not proud of everything I've done, Nell. I'll have penance from the Almighty, be sure of that. But if a little sleight of trickery in this cruel, hard world brought a smile to the working man and woman who can count on one hand the joys in their life..." More coughing, then winded breath, short and shallow. "Is...it wrong to want my epitaph...to be the laughter I brought? They're already erecting a statue of me—"

Now he was filling the room with children's happy faces and she'd not bear it.

"But it wasn't all magic, was it? Not for the animals. Not for *him*."

"Ah, Nell...animals die all the time for our amusement. Why is this creature the one you won't let me forget?"

"We made a deal not to speak of that night."

He reached out and clutched at her cloak, but she was having none of it.

"While I live," Barnum choked, brokenly.

"Nothing more."

"I hoped we'd part with you thinking of me...as a father."

"Father?" Nell angrily turned down the silver frame on the bed table. "You owned me!"

"Curse you, Little Eyes. You'd be in a cage in some roadside carnival if not for me, eating scraps tossed through the bars. I made you—" The sputtering fit returned, and Barnum meekly pointed for water. "—famous."

Nell was unmoved. Even dying, he was a bastard. "So as thanks, you want me to polish the memory of the great P. T. Barnum with lies."

"Nell—"

"Well, you spit before you shine. And I could, you know. Tell people what really happened that night. What would they think about the great Barnum then? Liar? Fraud? Maybe even call you a murderer?"

He tried to pull himself up. "It's him put you up to this, isn't it? What they say is true—you running after that English bastard. You may be one of God's misbegotten, Nell, but you're still a woman. And a fool if you think he can love anything but that elephant—"

"Jumbo." Nell bent low and hissed into his ear, "His name was Jumbo."

Damn it if what made Nell famous left her no match even for a dying old man pulling her close by the back of her neck, determined to exact a promise with the last of his earthly powers. But his eyes widened and he sobbed, wordlessly. When the convulsions came, she could see on his face the fear; he knew they'd be the last. Thank God. She fought his grip until the spasms stopped and his lungs slowly exhaled their final foulness against her cheek. Then Nell pulled free and tucked back the loosened curls of her wig, watching the lines smoothed from Barnum's face as his last shit stunk up the room. Crossed her mind to call someone. That wife of his. A doctor. But she didn't. Just clung to a hand going cold.

Then she wept and hated herself for it.

MRS. BARNUM ROSE FROM HER CHAIR WHEN NELL, SLIGHTLY dishevelled, stepped out of the room, could tell Death had come and gone. Look of a canary about her, not quite realizing she could fly away with those birds back there after Nell unlatched their cages, pushed open the window.

"Is that it?" Nell asked, seeing the round blue satin case, the clasp and trim of gold in the woman's hand.

Looking towards the door to her husband's room but taking no steps, the woman nodded.

Nell gave a tug to the bow under her chin securing her bonnet in place, took the case. "Then we're done, missus."

ACT I

THE QUALITY OF MERCY

Cape Breton, 1873

Watching those men on ladders unravel big blue letters down the side of Barnum's Menagerie and Circus tent, Nell figured painting a sign with her on it must have cost him a lot—even if she looked nothing like the toothy girl with the sunny ringlets and that name was one he'd given her. Maybe that's why nobody'd answer when she asked about going home to the highlands. Like Saturday nights when Mr. Penders scrubbed his neck and hands and came round with a bottle to see her Mam. Now he'd gone through all the bother getting the coal dust off so her mother couldn't say no, and Nell could go sit in the pumpkin leaves growing behind the shitter and keep company with Jesus until Mr. Penders quit grunting like the pigs.

Never took long. Mr. Penders lived in a shed back in the woods. His belly was big and hairy, and his moustache dropped off the sides of his mouth and disappeared under his chin, held onto the stink of kerosene and worms. When he talked, it was like his tongue'd come loose. Her Mam knew what he was on about, even if she didn't understand the words. Made sure his pocket always had a lemon sugar for Nell and he carved her shoes with pointy toes from a dead maple, painted with windmills and yellow swallows, like they were flying. But the shoes made some noise on the wooden floors of the church and those women coçooned in black, fast-moving lips and gnarled fingers wearing down rosary beads, were able to shush her without skipping a prayer.

Wrapping a kerchief about her head, her Mam observed Sundays to light candles, but only after mass was over. Less chance she'd get caught shaking coins out of the offertory box. Money's for the poor anyways, Mam'd say. Now you sit, like I told you, and wait quietly for the hand of God coming to fix you.

Nell imagined it'd be like a pinch, or maybe even a slap. Bible stories, if anything, weren't about being gentle. And would God ride a chariot through fire, or sidle up as some nice old man with a dog, an angel in disguise? While her Mam clutched her hands and closed her eyes, prayed the offal from her lust would disappear, Nell, tired of waiting, kicked off her wooden shoes and slipped silently around the outer aisles to look at the walls. The carved panels up there were very much like her shoes, bright yellows and etched birds flying, but no windmills, just soldiers with helmets beating Jesus and crowning him with thorns before nailing him to a cross. Lots of red paint. But the last picture wasn't even a carved panel.

Just, exquisite.

Two women, early morning but still dark, drawn to a light glowing from a cave. The older woman, kneeling, held open her arms, and from her happy-about-being-miserable look, Nell thought the woman was about to get her heart sucked out by the light. Nell's, too, the longer she looked. The younger, prettier woman was not looking into the glow but at Nell, same tired look on her face as her Mam got when Mr. Penders came round, clean neck and full bottle.

The painted image was so real, Nell felt that if she asked what those women were looking at, why, they'd tell her all about the good Lord inside that cave removing his shroud and ascending to Heaven. Her hand was just on its way out to touch as a big fleshy fist churned up her collar, yanked her backwards, held her up so that her shoeless feet dangled over the tips of polished black leather peeking from underneath a draping cassock. And being trussed up like that, Nell wasn't breathing so good.

Her Mam was clawing and scratching by the doors while the priest, whose luxurious grey-black hair rolled from his temples like harbour waves in winter, but whose eyes looked like they might pop right out of his head, called her a thieving Jezebel, stealing from the church, and Nell, the spawn of the devil. He tossed Nell into her Mam's arms and, if he had the power, into a pit of damnation. This house, he said, closing the doors on them, was a house of the Lord.

Damn shame what happened, because that house of the Lord was the only building that had a tin roof and wooden walls in what passed for a town. Most of the other houses had canvas walls that got rolled up in the summer when the air inside started to boil. But after the church burned to ashes, those ladies in black with hands on beads told anyone who'd listen, it was a miracle about that painting. Leaned up against a rock not far away, only thing saved by the hand of God.

Saved by someone, thought Nell without one bit of remorse.

About what happened next, she really didn't blame Mr. Penders too much. Maybe her Mam got things mixed up on account of not understanding his words. When he told Nell's mother, might be best to stop thinking about how the girl being born small as a doll was a curse but rather a blessing, her Mam got the idea to show Nell off at the market. Got Mr. Penders to stitch a sail into a tent and charged folks a penny to come inside.

Only, at first, no one cared to part with a hard-earned penny just to see Nell sniffling in the corner. Put them off their enjoyment. So, Mam rouged up Nell's cheeks with cinnabar and made her sing and poked at her with a stick until she danced. "'Tis But a Little Faded Flower" or "When the Corn is Waving, Annie Dear" soon had folks from far and wide lining up to see the tiny wonder, although whatever was in the rouge didn't make Nell feel so good. That's how Mademoiselle LeLacheur got wind of them.

Happy as a pig in shit when she poked her head through the canvas flaps and saw Nell pirouetting inside. Like she was trying hard not to show she'd found a gold coin right under their noses. Offering her Mam twice the price of admission, she asked to see Nell like the day she was born. Didn't care that Nell, turning around and bending over, no longer needed the paint to make her cheeks flush and kept staring at her when she and Mam talked low together in the corner, every now and then, Mam's eyes going wide. Next day, Mr. Penders started carving her a new pair of shoes. Nell thought she saw tears in the man's eyes while he worked but she wasn't sure. Never knew a man could cry.

Mam told Nell she was going on a trip to meet a great wizard who was going to make her grow like other girls. No, my dear, not for long, but only if she did all she was told. Mam wouldn't have to beat her anymore on account of folks saying, *Look what drinking with coal miners begets you,* and Nell wouldn't go sniffling in her secret place behind the shitter because crying only brought out the birch switch and not Jesus. She'd better not cry now because there'd been a great to-do to make all this happen and Mam wasn't having it. She kneeled and hugged Nell. First time she'd touched her since Nell was old enough to feed and dress herself. Mind your p's and q's, she said—one day she'd thank her Mam for sending her away—and she'd try not to be jealous that Nell got to see a place called New York City while Mam and Mr. Penders filled their lungs with coal dust.

Then Nell was put in a carriage with Mademoiselle LeLacheur, but not easily. Had to tie her hands and legs so she wouldn't spread like a snowflake. Do well, child, to mind me, the woman said, poking at Nell with her fingers like Nell once saw Mr. Penders do to a horse's mouth. Lots of brown crooked teeth. The woman, not Nell. Took the new shoes Mr. Penders made and tossed them out the carriage, and if Nell didn't stop snivelling, Mademoiselle LeLacheur would see to it that her arse wouldn't stand the touch of a feather cushion for a month.

After that, Mademoiselle didn't speak much, except when she pulled down the window and yelled to the driver, How much farther to Halifax? Ship was waiting, and if they missed it, the driver wouldn't know what hit him, by God. Everything ended in by God with Mademoiselle LeLacheur, as if she wanted everyone to know she was being put upon to do His work and would only be happy about it when she got rewarded in the next world. Stopped once to water the horses and for Nell to squat in the weeds. Mademoiselle tied a rope around her waist and held it so she wouldn't run off. When Nell got sick from the bumpy road and puked over the new pinafore her Mam had sewn for the occasion, Mademoiselle asked Jesus right out loud to tell her what was worse: Nell smelling so awfully bad or being forced to stick her head out the window and catch the grippe.

When town came, being no moon, Nell only heard it. Horses on the cobbles, timber masts creaking, bells clanging, slow like, back and forth, out in the harbour. A man singing about some woman he was best not knowing, but sad and far away, ending with a bilious hork. Sea air: salt and fish and soggy oakum. Went right onboard the ship and down into a cabin where Mademoiselle scrubbed Nell raw with some powerful soap in cold seawater poured into a basin and made her wash her clothes because, poor like her, they must be crawling with lice. Nell didn't care to have the woman staring at her while she was naked. First time Nell saw the look Mademoiselle gave her, she'd seen so often since: folks crossing themselves, thanking the good Lord they'd dodged whatever ailment or evil got her.

Sails unfurled and waves soon brushed against the hull. Men shouted and a bell dinged. Nell didn't see much beyond the peeling whitewash of the close cabin. Three bunks; the woman kept her on the top. Too far to crawl down, and even if she did, the door was locked. Wooden slats covering the ceiling. Rows of nine. Nell practiced her counting and her prayers. Be good and do what you're told. Nine plus nine was eighteen. The great wizard will fix you and send you home. Plus nine was twenty-seven. Don't be sinful thinking about getting shipwrecked or wishing rats under the bottom bed would eat Mademoiselle's face off.

In the morning, as the woman brushed her thinning white hair, she told Nell to mind her manners, seeing her staring at the cap she wore with someone else's brown curls stitched to the front. Then she tied Nell to the bunks while she went looking for a bucket so Nell could relieve herself. When the seas got rough, the bucket tipped and the dirty stuff sloshed across the floor.

For the rest of the voyage Mademoiselle sat on the bottom bunk, feet sticking out, shoes as tightly buttoned as the rest of her, and ran her fingers along tiny words in a pigskin-covered Bible. Every now and then she'd glare at Nell: "...in guilt was you born, and in sin your mother conceived you." And if Nell continued that caterwauling, she'd thrash her till she turned to butter.

THE BOAT NOW DOCKED, MADEMOISELLE FORCED NELL INTO AN empty flour sack and tied the opening with rope. No one was getting a look without paying, she said, by God. When Nell wailed and fought to be let out, the woman punched her and promised to drop her into the sea where she'd get swallowed by a whale if she wasn't quiet, and unlike Jonah, nothing would spit the likes of her out. So, Nell saw nothing of crowded New York Harbor, or horses pulling the carriage up Broadway, or the lobby of the St. Nicholas Hotel where someone was playing a piano.

After being swung around like a sack of potatoes, her head hanging down a man's back, who promised to carry the load uptown from the ship for two dollars, and whose rear end stunk like musty boiled cabbage, the sack was opened. Nell found herself wobbling on the edge of a desk in a room well lit by colossal windows overlooking crowded towers, and oversized sofas and chairs with polished rosewood arms carved with rosettes. Surrounding her, men who looked to normally be talking even if no one was listening but were now astonished with mouths stuck open mid-word.

"See? I told you." Mademoiselle nodded, fake curls wilting.

A man in a waistcoat slung with fobs was sitting behind the desk, pushed back by his ample girth, a ring of unruly hair about his head, jowls spreading over his tight collar. Old, except in the eyes. Grinning, he jumped up, limber as a schoolboy and, trembling with excitement, helped Nell step out of the flour sack pooled about her feet.

"How delightful!" The man, holding Nell's arms out, turned her around and around so that she got dizzy. "So tiny. And perfectly formed. Yes, amazing!"

On the other side of the desk the chorus of young, smartly dressed men with shiny hair, arms full of papers and ledgers, echoed his every sentiment.

"Another Feejee Mermaid?" jested one of the boys.

"No, lads, this is the real thing."

"Like I wrote you, Mr. Barnum," Mademoiselle LeLacheur had to get in there to say, "rare as an emerald. Won't find another like her, I'll dare to declare."

The old man's smile faded. "Will she grow?"

"No, Mr. Barnum. Child's mother swears it. Even had a doctor—"

"One of those British hacks up there?"

"A real American doctor."

"The child's mother?"

Mademoiselle pulled papers out of a cloth bag tied to her waist. "Signed 'em right there, see? Twenty-five dollars a week, just like you asked. Last you'll see of her, by God."

Nell didn't care for the sound of that and asked about going home. When Mr. Barnum laughed, those young men about him laughed too.

"My child! You are blessed! Everyone wants to be in my menagerie!"

Only Mademoiselle with the pretend curls wasn't laughing. Maybe for a moment, she was even biting her lip.

THE GIRL WITH THE GOLDEN HAIR

New York City, 1875

Letters from Nell's mother, written in her big, childish scrawl, arrived regularly in those early years, always wanting money—what she got paid from Mr. Barnum for schooling her daughter, as she put it, not nearly enough to keep hodgepodge simmering in the pot. Mam insisted her daughter owed her because her own life was a misery of sweet-talking miners and unwanted bastards, and she could have gotten rid of Nell if she'd gone to that doctor in Sydney, but she was a Christian. No mention of whatever became of Mr. Penders, but it didn't sound like he was carving any more wooden shoes. Nell was thankful reading and writing came easy to her because if she didn't reply, and her Mam stopped asking, who'd send her a letter or wonder how she was doing? She liked tucking away inside that if someone asked: yes, she did have a mother, somewhere, and made up stories about how much Mam loved and missed her. But no one ever asked.

In one of those letters, Mam wrote about a valley she'd moved to, how in the spring it rained pink apple blossoms, but when she died, the letter asking Mr. Barnum to pay for her funeral came from Glace Bay, where miners tunnelled under the ocean for coal and probably didn't have much call for apple trees. Nell wanted to go, and Mr. Barnum was so very sorry for her, but Nell being who she was, everyone would want to see her without paying and that wouldn't be right to the memory of her poor, dear Mam. Besides, there were the matinees and evening shows to consider.

Truth be told, Nell had little time to miss her mother. There was much about her that needed making up. Barnum regaled his boys of the press, as he called them, with a fanciful tale of little Nell's birth in 1858, making her five years older than she was. So often was the lie told, even Nell came to believe it. Barnum figured the extra years made her stature even more remarkable. And no one was to ever know her real name. Things like names got you into trouble with church records and family members. Nothing was to get in the way of his creating Little Eyes Nell Kelly. The one and only. The tiniest, most perfectly formed woman in the world. Her size due, Barnum claimed, to her mother taking a fright inside The House of the Seven Gables. Nell's Mam never read a book in all her days, but it was a favourite of the first Mrs. Barnum, who'd stayed in bed for ten years. It must have been a long book.

At first, a collie on hind legs pushed Nell in a baby carriage each performance until he bit her during the bear parade. Left a scar and Nell had to sit alone for days in a saddler's wagon just in case the dog turned mad. It didn't occur to her until later that if she'd started foaming at the mouth, they'd have shot her too.

Then, she rode in a tiny wagon pulled by two clowns dressed like a horse while she sang, *Beside the grave of Jennie dear / I sit tonight and weep / The Lamps of love are lit on high / The world is hush'd to sleep*. Another clown dressed like a cat followed her around playing a fiddle. A little too close for comfort. Started licking her neck when he thought no one was looking.

She was relieved then, when Elephant Bill led Bucephalus across the ring, told her to get on. *Little Eyes Nell Kelly. The World's Smallest Singing, Dancing, Horse-riding Woman and Her Ring of Fire.* The last bit was kind of a stretch. Bucephalus was an old Shetland pony as gentle as a puppy. For two years they rode together, Bucephalus dutifully stopping on cue so Nell could step through a wooden ring covered in orange and yellow crepe paper fanned to look like flames. Time spent with the old pony made Nell wish less for a place that rained apple blossoms. Every performance she got up on the saddle, she'd lean over, pat him, and whisper, We're stuck in this together, so let's make the best of it, my sweet boy! But then he started coughing and plodded and wheezed around the ring. Nell pleaded with Barnum to get a doctor and he said, There, Little Eyes, of course we'll take care of the beast. Each day she brought Bucephalus an apple. If he ate the apple, she'd lead him out of the stable. The doctor never came and the cough worsened and the pony soon couldn't make it around the ring. Unable to sleep, Nell crept into Bucephalus's stall before her usual hour and surprised the keeper as he was putting a bullet into the pony's head. *Kerplunk.* Down he went at her feet.

Nell didn't scream, she didn't cry, didn't make a sound. Just snuck back to her bed and lay there, not singing for her supper, trying to keep her eyes open so she wouldn't dream of that sweet horse, wondering why she didn't stop that man with the rifle, until Barnum came for a sit. Grandfatherly Barnum. The consoling old man who'd lived a long time and understood what his young favourite must be feeling. Had he not known loss in his life? Of course he had! He once had the greatest museum of oddities in America, and watched it burn to the ground. Started over! Nell had a big heart, Barnum could see that, and he didn't want her to suffer, but probably best not to get too attached to anything, especially an animal. Not in this life, not for someone like her. After all, the circus was her home now and he was her guardian. Be a trouper, he said. Everyone in the circus *must* perform, until they couldn't.

THE NEWSPAPERS PRINTED THE STORY BEFORE ANYONE IN THE CIRCUS caught wind of the plans. Barnum was to exhibit Nell in London.

What about the long lines of ticket-buying patrons in New York? His business partners fumed and stomped. Was now the best time to leave the country?

But the mercurial Barnum knew, much as he had done years before with his celebrated General Tom Thumb, the patronage of Buckingham Palace would make Nell a phenomenon in the eyes of Americans, who didn't want a monarch, just a monarch's approval.

A series of exhibitions was arranged, and the relentless onslaught of publicity began even before sailing from New York City.

Nell trembled with anticipation while packing for the trip. England! Surely this was the great wizard's promised spell at last, even if she no longer believed in magic. A kindly word from the Queen, and everyone would see Nell as much more than an oddity in a menagerie.

If only her Mam could have seen the tiny gold-painted carriage bringing Nell to the Egyptian Hall in Piccadilly. Dressed as Marie Antoinette, a frantically flapping budgie trapped in a birdcage topping her towering white wig, she alighted under the stone gaze of Isis and Osiris in high relief over columned doors and waved shyly as hired men clasping arms held back the screaming throng desperate to see the world's tiniest woman.

Mr. Barnum's pixie dust sprinkled in the *Times* had worked.

Patrons in the grand hall were treated to fanciful tableaus where Nell figured as the Empress Josephine and the lead-white Queen Elizabeth. Children scurried onstage, getting measured, giggling over being taller. Often Nell sang with a voice Barnum billed as sweeter than even his great Swedish Songbird, Jenny Lind, accompanied by flutes and violins and dancing girls swirling thin veils. Best Nell could do was carry a tune, but by the time anyone concurred, they'd already paid.

Each performance concluded with Barnum playing ventriloquist with Nell upon his lap, his fingers woven into her corset stays.

"Is it true, Nell Kelly, that the handsome young men in the audience can purchase your photograph?"

"Yes, Mr. Barnum. Only twenty shillings."

"I see. And what do they get when they make the purchase?"

"A receipt, Mr. Barnum."

"A receipt?"

"Yes, a kiss on the lips."

Barnum then invited the wealthiest of patrons into a private salon where Nell, clad in a grey-white body stocking, her face painted to match, posed provocatively in the manner of a classical Greek nude, allowing closer and more personal observation, along with the offerings of cake and champagne. Yes, yes, he would say, I'm a temperance man, but it'd be rude not to provide some refreshment to my guests.

All this, three performances a day, seven days a week. The takings beyond anyone's wildest expectations. And Nell, powdering her face and lacing herself into heavy, tight-fitting costumes, surrounded by her own smiling image on posters, immured herself from Barnum's fingers drumming into the skin of her back while she sat on his lap or watching his head animal handler, Elephant Bill, taking pleasure beating the horses while staring at her like he'd not eaten in days. Her only respite came on Sundays, for even though her performances continued, hungry Bill disappeared, returning in the morning smelling of gin and stale rosewater while the God-fearing showman took to his hotel room with a Bible. Adverse to making money on a Sunday, Barnum had no problem with Nell making it for him.

Indeed, the much-hoped-for silver-edged summons to Buckingham Palace arrived in the gloved hand of a footman. None too soon, after a thousand pounds of expense, reckoned the showman. Nell practised her curtsy. Her nervous stomach emptied the wrong way all on its own. Barnum spent a hundred pounds more to dress her in billowing velvet with crimson and gold trim. A genuine diamond tiara was tucked into her wig.

Why, the Queen's just like a regular lady, Nell was thinking, trying to hide the smile in her reflection in the polished marble floor as she bowed deeply and perfectly when presented to Her Majesty Victoria, her son Leopold, and the Princess Royal. As Nell rose elegantly from her curtsy, the royal poodle, slipping and snarling across the glossy floor of the picture gallery, spilled her over, latching onto the folds of her dress. The more she tugged, the more the poodle yapped and pulled, tiara coming loose, curls dropping from their pins. The prince gallantly chased after the dog, hairpiece now in its mouth, Nell in pursuit, under the indifferent visages of dead kings and their consorts, rather much to the amusement of the Queen.

ACT II

CASUALTIES OF WAR

Madison Square Garden, 1881

If Nell had a friend, that'd be Dora. She wore suspenders and black-and-white overalls and was the back half of a heifer in a skit about the cow running away with a spoon, but she was always dragging her hooves. She came running over to Nell's railcar when she saw James Bailey, what hair was left pooling around his chin, leading Elephant Bill and a group of fellows carrying ladders. Mostly because Dora just liked to know what most folks didn't want her to, but everyone in the circus knew Barnum's partner was the one giving out bad news to performers and getting rid of sick animals.

"Like I tell you, Nell—you flitting about like there's no tomorrow—tomorrow always comes."

Workmen brushed whitewash over Nell's name and the girl with the golden ringlets on the canvas sign hanging on the side of her railcar. In her place, the outline of an elephant. A very large elephant.

Bill grinned from where he was overseeing, winked at Nell.

"Mr. Barnum wanted you to be older just so's folks think you're more special." Dora sounded pleased. "Now you're just long in the tooth for an ingenue around here."

No! Thousands of people still shouted *We love you, Nell* at every performance. Children adored her. And hadn't Barnum talked about an even greater London venture only a month ago? One that would include the continent? Yet, when she could find words, all Nell heard in them was defeat.

"But...Mr. Barnum's already got lots of elephants."

"I heard it cost ten thousand dollars. Can you even imagine so much money? Set me up in one of those Park Avenue mansions with an indoor bath and hot water. I'd bathe till I looked like a prune." Dora twirled elegantly as if the bottom of her cow costume had a long silk train. "You'll see. Next season, everyone'll be asking, Nell who?"

Dora wanted slapping, but her truth felt like it was snaking down Nell's throat and swallowing her heart.

"Ah, now don't you be listening to Dora's tales, Miss Nell." Mr. Bailey tipped his hat by way of good day. "You'll always have a place here."

Tusks were drawn on the canvas, eventually to be gleaming white, and looking half a mile long, with a howdah carrying a dozen smiling, waving children.

"But why's this elephant so special?"

"That's Jumbo. The largest, most dangerous African elephant in the world, and the most famous. He will be, anyway, when Mr. Barnum gets done—and if he doesn't kill somebody."

That was Mr. Bailey's way of asking if Nell would be so good as to move out of her private railcar. Mr. Barnum wanted it refurbished for Jumbo and his keeper. Nell could bunk in the clown wagon with Dora and the others.

NO ONE KNEW FOR CERTAIN IF DOC MURPHY WAS A REAL DOCTOR. To him, curing a toothache meant a swig of rum and rusty pliers. Still, what the circus doctor told Nell about dosing an elephant with a purgative rang true. Taking a barrelful didn't seem like something Nell could get away with. Not that she meant this new elephant harm, just enough shit to get those fine la-de-da ladies coming to Hippodrome shows turning blue, running this way and that, looking for the commodes. Mr. Barnum would have to ship that shitty elephant right back to England. Then that sign'd get painted over and Nell'd be back, better than ever. Bigger than that elephant. She even had ideas for a new act because she had to show them, show them all. Elephants can't sing. Elephants can't dance. And Nell knew what happened to performers and animals no one wanted to see anymore. They got left behind. Or worse. And with her Mam long dead, where would she go? Made her hate that elephant even more.

Jumbo. Jumbo. Jumbo. Hearing nothing but Jumbo, and she heard lots.

Mostly from that young fella, Lew. One of Barnum's men, always in tow doing something halfway between bowing and genuflecting. Llewelyn or Llewellyn. Barnum kept tripping over all those Ls, so he cut them down. Nice enough kid. Lanky and couldn't see past his nose without thick glasses. Pant legs cut above the ankle. Lew said his mother got tired of brushing the city's mud and dung out of the bottom of his trousers, so she took scissors to 'em.

He'd taken a shine to Nell. At first, mostly out of curiosity when she'd come to see Mr. Barnum or when Lew dogged his master around overseeing the circus. Guess he was surprised that Nell could be like a normal woman, but the kid was mighty green about the circus. And women. Nell never figured his affections—more like affectations—were serious. Lew didn't give off that he even wanted to know how a young fella woos a sweetheart, and no doubt his mother would have dropped in an apoplectic fit if she thought her lad had taken up with a circus freak.

Considering how Barnum liked his flattering young bucks of the hothouse flower type—loud and bright colours—Nell thought it a bit unusual when she heard Lew was favoured to go to England with Elephant Bill and Jim Davis, Barnum's shipping agent, to bring back Jumbo. Maybe even felt sorry for him. No one much liked being around the head trainer and that elephant cost an honest-to-God fortune. Shipping an animal that size in the hold of a boat? Anything could go wrong, so there'd be hell to pay, and most times Lew didn't get through a day without stumbling over his own feet.

But no denying the kid was a maestro with words, and Nell, sweetly, encouraged him to write her every day from London. If

Lew knew he was being used to gather intelligence on her enemy, he gallantly never let on. He also wrote most of those circus stories in the newspapers Barnum laid claim to. His job was to keep Jumbo in print, both sides of the ocean. Didn't matter if the stories were a bit stretched, or even just plain made up, as long as folks talked. And folks talking reached into a pocket a whole lot easier for the price of admission. But Lew had his work cut out for him. Right from the start, sounded like there was trouble in England over that elephant.

"Those British lords are demanding their parliament not sell Jumbo to a Yankee," Lew wrote Nell. "Be the War of Independence all over again."

His eagerly awaited letters from London were long and descriptive, with rarely a kind word for anything British. The Atlantic crossing had almost killed him. Ship doctor said, one more day and the kid would have been coughing up lungs. Practically kissed the dock in London. Not that he got a lick of sympathy from Elephant Bill. And Mr. Davis only cared about the numbers in his ledger and meeting sailing times.

As for London, Lew hated the city he saw little of, on account of refusing to get on anything that moved. Oily-brown sun—lightened up some around midday—through air stinging of sulfur, stinking of fresh-caught eels, privies, and stewing chimney pots, gagging the back of your throat, burning your eyes stumbling down choking winding narrow lanes clogged with wagons and carriages tossing mud if you weren't mindful to dodge their wheels, snarling dogs and rattling, clattering, ringing omnibuses. Boys with runny noses and rheumy eyes chewing off chunks of onions and potatoes and wiping their mouths with greasy forearms, nice as pie, yes sir, why of course sir, you'll be wanting to go down that lane, take you where you want to go, then steal you blind. And those ladies in muslin, porcelain-white hands covered in kid, while women in made-over dresses stained with sweaty yellow looked boldly right at you, called you lovie, and hawked bread and flowers from makeshift stalls they'd just as easily squat behind to relieve themselves. Men, shoving you this way and that, same blank-eyed gaze as the horses with foaming mouths dragging heavy wagons over what might have been red cobbles under admirals looking down from columns.

Not the London Nell had seen from a gold carriage.

Jumbo's home, wrote Lew, was in the London Zoological Gardens. Tucked in the corner of Regent's Park, ruled by autocratic Superintendent Abraham Bartlett of the London Zoological Society. Small man, white beard, frock coat brushed every morning. Never set foot outside without his high beaver hat and, considering the pigeons and swallows nesting in the rafters of the Elephant House, Lew didn't think that wise. Bartlett made no secret of his disdain for the Americans, but Mr. Barnum's bank draft got deposited right quickly. And for all his airs and graces, turns out the superintendent was no more than a barber's son who'd taught himself everything he knew about animals by stuffing dead ones for the libraries of rich dukes.

Abraham Bartlett was also, as Lew plainly put it, as crooked as an Irish copper, which really didn't sound that bad to Nell, but what did she know.

If anything gave Barnum pause as to the haste in which the London Zoo took his low offer to buy Jumbo—a rare, in-captivity African elephant, aggressive and notoriously hard to train, yet loved by children, and their children, who rode on his back for almost twenty years—he never said. But Lew had concerns over what the superintendent had done, and Elephant Bill shared them.

Jumbo's irascible rages in the months before the offer came from the circus left the superintendent worrying that captivity had brought about the early onset of musth. Boys ran behind Jumbo on his daily walks about the zoo, carrying a tarpaulin that could be unfurled quickly should the elephant sprout a ten-foot erection, but the real concern was his temper. Jumbo nightly thrashed about his pen in the Elephant House, snapping oak beams and cracking brick walls.

Adding bracing was becoming a daily chore for the carpenters. What if he raged during a crowded afternoon in the zoo?

The only person who stood between this kind of disaster and Jumbo was his keeper, Matthew Scott. A soft-spoken, solitary fellow, not much in the way of book learning, who hadn't left the elephant's side in close to twenty years. No one else could handle Jumbo and his keeper knew it, and although Lew didn't say, both he and Elephant Bill guessed that Scott had no intention of letting his beloved charge be sold to the Americans, not when they were clearly lords of the manor here in London.

Now, because of the delays, missed sailings, the ever-growing tearful and angry crowds at the zoo, wailing children, speeches in Parliament, pleas from Her Majesty, thousands of letters to newspapers, editorials, and Jumbo prostrating himself in chains while Scott was cheered, Lew wrote one word: *Jumbomania*. And Abraham Bartlett got the brunt of it. Selling London's beloved Jumbo made him the most hated man in England. But Lew inferred, selling the elephant was the only way to get rid of a potentially dangerous animal and a keeper who no longer knew his place.

Jumbo be damned, vowed Elephant Bill, itching to make the English backside of that elephant bleed with his bullhook. He'd have Jumbo in that shipping crate and at the dock, sure as shit, mark his words. No more theatrics.

But in one of Lew's final letters to Nell, he confided that Barnum himself was orchestrating the delay through daily telegraphs, filing Chancery lawsuits against the Society to thwart his own sale, penning hateful anti-American articles in the press, all to stoke anticipation across the Atlantic where Jumbo would be a sensation the minute he set foot in America.

THE MONARCH'S BUTTERFLY

Castle Garden Pier, 1882

On the day Jumbo arrived in New York City, Nell sang three songs in the Hippodrome show: "Somebody's Coming, But I'll Not Tell Who," "Send for Mother, Birdie's Dying," and "Never Take the Horseshoe from the Door," in an act called Bring Our Lady Liberty Home! Every American's patriotic duty to dig into their pockets to help the French erect that giant statue on Bedloe's Island was addressed by Mr. Barnum before each performance.

Nell wore a crown and held a torch while two horses blackened with boot polish pranced around the ring, pulling a wagon decorated with red, white, and blue bunting. Her songs weren't French or even remotely appropriate to the cause, but the cheering crowd didn't seem to mind. Flowing robes concealed Nell strapped in behind the driver to keep her standing if the horses bolted. This evening, she got through her songs so fast that Hoo Hoo Hanlan had a hard time keeping up on the banjo and danced like his feet weren't attached to his legs just so's folks wouldn't notice.

"You got a fire to go to?" he asked crankily when the horses pulling them out of the ring were taken hold of by their handler.

Nell just handed him her torch and crown, tried not to think about one day being no more important to the circus than a fiddle player.

Dora was waiting as arranged, woollen trousers and cotton shirt hung over her arm. "Got what you wanted, like you asked. Seventy-five cents, mind you. Two bits extra for what I had to do to get 'em. Now, you gonna tell me why?"

Nell thanked her friend, but not so good a friend that Dora let Nell have the bunk above her when she moved back into the clown wagon. Nell found out the hard way what happens in the bottom bunk.

Wide-eyed Hoo Hoo stayed around to watch Nell peel off her robe.

"Sweet Helen of Troy! You're not changing right here?"

Had to, and Dora wouldn't understand why the rush.

But she could guess. "Nell Kelly, are you sneakin' around for a man?" She laughed like a donkey. "I told you, no regular Joe's gonna stay longer than it takes to do ya. And a mighty strange one if he wants you dressed looking like a fella."

Nell shoved her curls under the boy's cap Dora handed her. "You forgetting about Elephant Bill?"

Dora looked away, bit her lip. "No...but he's no man, Nell, not that one."

The zebras were finishing their turn around the Hippodrome. Skittish bastards at the best of times. Dora jumped out of their way. When they'd passed, Nell was gone; Iowa Jim was waiting for her on Broadway. Claimed he was part or half Sioux, ran away from some tongue twister place called Saskatchewan. Come to ride in Barnum's Indian show—painted-up warriors, trick riding, shooting arrows—but after he shot one of the best riders in the leg, cleaning out the animal cages was all they'd let him do. He was a tall one for sixteen; Nell'd see all kinds of things from up on those shoulders.

"You still set on going to the docks? Pretty rough down there, Miss Nell."

"Gotta see for myself. Besides, people'll think I'm your little brother up here. Mr. Barnum says Jumbo'll be a big star, maybe his biggest."

"Not one bigger than you." Then Iowa Jim grinned. He did have a nice set of teeth. "Okay, bigger, but not more famous."

LEW HAD DONE HIS JOB WELL. ALL OF NEW YORK CITY WAS PUSHING and shoving for a first look at Jumbo, maybe even hoping for a glimpse of his famed temper. What a sight that would be! Those tusks of his sweeping folks into the harbour. Dead bodies left, right, and centre. Too bad Lew never got to see the river clogged with boats, tugs spraying plumes of water, the smoke and sirens and bells. Three miles off the coast, the kid's body stitched into canvas was quietly dropped into the sea. Worst case of seasickness the captain ever saw.

The pier was crowded under April rain, more like wet snow. So much shoving and shouting, children crying, toppling mountains of suitcases and trunks, jostling bread and fruit carts, a buggy pushed into the water by the Castle Garden rotunda. Some boys peeled off coats and jumped in, tried to save the horse, but their fingers turned to ice and they couldn't loosen the harness. The dripping owner kept saying, who's going to pay who's going to pay, and for a while it looked like those blue coats on horseback trying to settle folks down might get pushed in the water too.

Iowa Jim shouted for Nell to hold on as they were swept along to the waterfront, trying for a glimpse of tugs nudging the *Assyrian Monarch* along the wharf. Biting snow now back to a heavy rain, cold seeping right through wool and scarves. Way too miserable for any more standing around and waiting. When those gangways were lowered, folks pushed their way onboard, beaten by sailors with clubs and truncheons, boys scrambling into the rigging, others hand over fist up ropes on the ship's side.

"The damned British tried to keep Jumbo from us—not anymore!" Iowa Jim easily got caught up in a red-coated frenzy that, until that morning, he'd known nothing about. If Nell wasn't on his shoulders, he'd be storming the vessel too, hell-bent on British plunder. "Look! Jumbo's howdah!"

Twirling as it was lowered to the dock, still lettered with *London Zoo*.

Then came thundering and cheering and clapping and the crowding clutter of tugs and steamers blasting horns and whistles. Jumbo in a wooden box was pulled from the hold and hung from the barge crane. Iowa Jim got fiercely elbowed, searched the crowd for revenge. Nell covered her ears. A man climbing higher in the ship's rigging for a better look lost his grip and plunged, spinning like a wagon wheel, with a piercing one-note cry, into the water, then hoorah! hoorah! when he surfaced and waved.

Jumbo, terrified by the noise and the swinging of his crate, torturously roaring, dangled between ship and dock, his trunk thrashing wildly through the opening. White froth splashing about the rocking barge.

"Why don't they lower him to the dock?"

"Put Jumbo down! Dear God, put Jumbo down!"

"Don't like how this crowd's getting." Iowa Jim's hands tightened about Nell's ankles. "Not for me, Miss Nell, I can take care of myself, but if you fall, well...I don't want to think about what might happen—"

A sharp, loud crack silenced the crowd. Windblown water spilled against hulls of boats. Rain pelting. Hands pointed up. Iron cables chaffed and squeaked against oak.

"That crane'll break for sure." Iowa Jim sounded almost dazzled by the hope of it.

A woman shrieked as a man jumped from the deck of the *Assyrian Monarch* onto the front of the swaying elephant in the box. Nell held her breath, considered reciting one of those useless prayers of Mam's that never got answered—then again, might be best for all of them if that crane did break.

"He and that elephant gonna end up in the river. God damn fool."

The curse startled Nell, seeing as how Iowa Jim once told her his parents didn't believe in sparing the rod. He'd run off to the circus to escape their Pentecostal beatings, but Jim always sounded like he was at Sunday dinner. Even when he fell off that horse a few months later and got dragged around the ring, head bouncing off all those metal bars, worst he said was *golly* just before they pulled a sheet of canvas over his toothless face.

The man calming Jumbo was small, his moustache bushy, and when his hat snapped off in the wind, he briefly looked to mourn it. He secured Jumbo's trunk under one arm, held onto the wooden beams, and leaned his forehead against the elephant's face. Jumbo immediately settled in his wooden crate and the swinging began to stop.

The crowd shouted and clapped and whistled. *Hooray!*

"That must be Mr. Scott, Jumbo's keeper." Iowa Jim now had Nell bouncing around on his shoulder.

Looking down from the dangling crate, the man waved timidly, then more forcefully as applause and cheers greeted their arrival on American soil.

TORCHES FLARED AGAINST NIGHT AS JUMBO GOT LOADED ONTO THE wagon, his keeper still clinging to the front of the crate, the elephant's trunk hugging his waist. Horse harnesses jingled being strapped into place. Whips snapped. Men barked. Dogs barked. Crowds from the docks flooded streets, filled alleys, spilled onto rooftops, hung from windows. The hard white bits of cabbage heads, split and dripping tomatoes, and carrots got tossed just for the fun of it from the hands of snotty, long-haired toughs, running along in the downpour. Nell's breath steamed in that numbing chill.

Welcome Jumbo, The Great Jumbo, Britain's Loss America's Gain, Jumbo Lord of Beasts: letters, bleeding in the rain, hung limp from poles.

Nell was sorry she had to squeeze the boy's head to see over the crowd. "Poor man, he looks chilled to the bone."

"Why Miss Nell, you sweet on Jumbo's keeper? Ouch!"

Iowa Jim thought it was a good idea, Nell bringing the umbrella, but in pulling Jim's hair, it fell and was trampled under boots.

Outside of Castle Garden Pier, the river of muck pouring down State Street sucked in the wheels of the heavily loaded wagon. Wet and stinging cold and boredom dulled cheers and chants under the hard splash of rain. Jumbo wailed plaintively, rocking inside his wooden confines. Hard to wish harm on a creature coming into New York City pretty much like she did. Bigger only meant bigger the box.

Barnum's carriage arrived well after midnight, horse and wheels sliding through mud. One of his partners, James Hutchinson, sat with him. He'd be worried about their investment. Elephant Bill grimly hung off the back. Iowa Jim, shoving in closer, gagged when Nell's tightening hands almost stopped his breathing. Sounded as if there was talk of freeing Jumbo and letting him walk the rest of the way. Mr. Hutchinson shook his head and crossed his hands. Not having a wild elephant running amok in Manhattan.

Barnum stuck his head out of the carriage and waved his cane.

"Tickets to see Jumbo's first matinee for every man and boy who puts his back into it!"

Jackets and caps and coats got peeled off and handed to wives, girlfriends, and mothers. The seeping sky let loose. Ropes tied to the wagon were drawn ahead of the horses to help the animals pull. Hundreds of men, wet-soaked faces, grunting, cursing, shouldered in behind.

"Look, there she goes!" Iowa Jim sounded sad at missing the fun.

At the sucking sound of wheels pulled from mud and the wagon again rocking slowly towards Broadway, thousands swelled around and behind, fists rapping and banging against the side of the crate, terrifying Jumbo, no one hearing his English keeper pleading for them to stop.

At the overhead train tracks, Elephant Bill climbed on top of the crate, got down on hands and knees. Pigeons awake now, blinking white and wet, streaking across the dark grey dawn. "Two inches. She'll clear it by two inches."

Chief and Gypsy, circus elephants herded down from the Madison Square Garden Hippodrome, whipped and prodded by Elephant Bill and his boys, shouldered against the backside of Jumbo's crate. The wagon slowly lurched underneath the raised train tracks, then beyond, between canyons of candlelit tenements, windows darkened by sleepy faces pressing glass, wondering at this dream where marshy streets steamed with the shit of elephants.

IOWA JIM PULLED NELL FROM HIS SHOULDERS OUTSIDE THE FOURTH Avenue entrance to Madison Square Garden and rubbed his stiff muscles. His woman was a motherly Chinese contortionist with tiny feet, and he was anxious to get to the warm bed she'd have waiting. Nell sheltered in a doorway, watching as Mr. Barnum, satisfied his precious cargo was in safe hands, jovially invited Bailey and Hutchinson to join him in a late dinner or early breakfast as they scurried under umbrellas. Rain pelted the canvas Elephant Bill ordered pulled over Jumbo's crate, while some of the circus boys on ladders peeled off the doors and the fanlight over the entrance to the Hippodrome. But heads shook. The crate was still too large to pass.

"Ah, leave it till dawn. Get a few hours' sleep, boys." Elephant Bill rapped the side of Jumbo's crate with his fist, shaking out his wet hat.

He couldn't see Nell huddled in the doorway, pointing her hand at him as if it held a gun. She could do it, shoot him, if she had one, but she could never find one small enough, one that didn't drag her hand down when she fired or knock her off her feet. Might miss him altogether or shoot someone else by mistake. Maybe even Jumbo. Two birds with one shot.

"Follow me, English. I'll get you a bed and supper."

But Jumbo's keeper wasn't having any of that. Nell stepped back into the shadows, the mewling, mournful howls from inside the box loud above the pelting rain. Matthew Scott grabbed hold of one of the men's pry bars and stabbed in and out of Jumbo's flailing trunk at the boards at the front of the crate, being rocked by the elephant sensing his weeks of confinement were at end.

"Come on, lads, help me get him out!"

No one moved.

"Not going near that monster," shouted one of Elephant Bill's men.

Rain poured off Scott's drawn face. He pulled at the boards like a man possessed, hampered by Jumbo's trunk trying to wrap itself around his head, rain washing blood off his hands. This was no keeper and his charge. Nell'd seen lots of men with elephants. This man's gaze, fiery, unnatural, yet she couldn't turn from it. Imagine someone working like that to free you. Must care a great deal. Not normal. Nell thought from his heaving shoulders, the slowing of the pry bar's jabs, if Scott stopped, he'd collapse from exhaustion right there. But he couldn't stop. The crate was solid and the oak timbers and pine boards cracked and splintered slowly. All the while, the keeper's words to Jumbo were soft and encouraging. Nell wanted to hear them. She wanted to get closer. But enough of the wood broke away and Jumbo began pushing his way out.

He was big. Massive. Those nearby pushed and shoved each other as they stepped back. Men on the ladders over the entrance scrambled down and ran across the street. For once, Barnum had not been tooting his own horn. Larger than any elephant in the circus, and with him came the foul stench of confinement that threatened to turn the stomachs of men used to the stink of sick and ill-kept animals. Jumbo delicately stabbed at ground that did not move in front of him. First one foot out, then the other, heavy grey skin in folds, coated in thick, reeking filth, blood oozing from the base of his two white nubs. Not the great sweeping arcs of ivory painted on the signs. His keeper, panting, spent, sank to his knees as the elephant's trunk reached up and looked to pull down a piece of wet New York City sky to wrap about them.

Nell slipped amongst the men filling the inner passageway, carrying rifles and bullhooks, wet hair plastered to faces, trousers and shirts dripping and steaming, and yelling, clamouring performers tugging on decency over lack of bedclothes, running here and there, shouting, *Watch out! Stay back!* Word was dashed off to Messrs. Barnum, Bailey, and Hutchinson—come quick! Jumbo was entering the Hippodrome! Snorting and bellowing, ears fanning, walking unsurely behind his keeper, a great monolithic shadow lurking over them all.

Then he stopped.

"Jumbo?" His keeper, concerned, tried to coax the elephant forward.

But Jumbo remained motionless, then groaned, loud and long. Nell, like so many others, gasped at the pitiful sight of him sinking to his knees with a rolling growl, to lie motionless under trapeze ropes, lights, and rows and rows of empty seats circling him.

Nell had never heard such silence in a place erected for thousands.

"Mr. Scott! Mr. Scott, what's wrong with him?" Barnum pulled the dinner cloth from his neck and daubed his forehead as the giant's legs began to twitch.

But Nell, who peered into the ring through the legs of others because who'd notice a little boy, said, but loudly, "He wants to stretch."

His keeper, who'd thrown himself down by Jumbo's side, and who'd heard, glared at her, bewildered and maybe even angry, like she knew something he should. Elephant Bill yelled for someone to get that damn kid out of here, but no one paid any mind. The circus's new star attraction, the most expensive animal in the world, looked to be dying mere hours after his arrival, right there in the middle of the Hippodrome, and thousands of tickets already sold.

"Oh my! Our ten thousand dollars!" Mr. Hutchinson's voice was high and choked.

Then, slowly, Jumbo began rocking and scratching his back against the rough floor, snorting, rolling from one side to the other, puffs of sand blowing everywhere, cheers and hoorays when he slowly lumbered to his feet.

"Well done!" cheered Barnum.

Mr. Hutchinson by his side, looking as if he might need to sit.

But Nell was fixed on Elephant Bill: big smile, putting his arm around Matthew Scott's shoulder, pulling him aside friendly like, and leaning in, added, "I said leave him in the rain. You get a mind to disobey me again, English, choose the part of hell you'll be on the next boat to."

Then he ordered the man to lead Jumbo to his stall, where leg irons were snapped in place and stakes drove briefly-tasted freedom deeply into the ground.

THE SHOW DOES GO ON

Madison Square Garden, 1882

No performer was going to admit a new attraction might get more attention, but all morning a steady stream of curious came, shrugged, and left.

"Aren't you dolled up, Miss Nell." Nala was side-eyeing Jumbo. Towering Jumbo. "Makes me wonder why, dressing so fine to see an elephant." Nala always asked questions she didn't want an answer to.

Nell was just showing everyone who was still the biggest attraction. That's all. Certainly not looking to see his keeper, who was nowhere to be found, although Jumbo had been scrubbed clean.

"Don't see what the fuss is about." Nala took a bite out of a bun. She liked them sweet, and her teeth were black. "I mean, elephants are supposed to be big, aren't they? Compared to you."

A snake charmer by profession, Nala carried no snake that morning and had her Medusa hair wrapped in curling papers. Zip, whom everyone called Pinhead, stood beside her. Mostly he was called Nala's dog because he was always by her side and when he spoke, it sounded like a kind of yipping. He had a very tiny head with bristly hair razored to a point. Barnum claimed he was from the jungles of Borneo, but no one ever came from where Barnum said, and Zip sounded like he was from Alabama. He was staring at Jumbo munching on beetroot, washing it down with slurping and splashing gulps of water, all the while letting go an almost constant stream of piss from an embarrassingly large penis. Zip rolled his eyes and led Nala away by the hand.

But as Nell quickly discovered, though she tried in vain to resist, if you stared into Jumbo's impenetrable eyes long enough, it got hard not to. Impossible not to wonder how this strange world, this pantheon of mirth, must seem to him. Burnt-sugary air and smoky paraffin and kerosene, faces painted with ochre-tinged lard, rustling canvas walls, night and day whining and grunting, roars and squeals and chirps from cages and pens, damnation this and fuck you that, and the slop buckets splashing into poorly drained latrines.

Jumbo plucked an apple out of a nearby barrel and, with a *phoot phoot,* offered it, clutched in the tip of his trunk.

"Little girl, stand back!" His keeper, fearfully, as he unwrapped himself from the stained calico blanket he'd slept under, pulled bits of straw from his mouth. "Oh."

Nell was in blue satin striped with gold, wearing her best gloves, fringe on her bustle.

"Madam…miss…goodness." The man didn't know where to look. "I thought you were a child."

Nell watched as the man dug through the straw for his coat and hastily pulled it on. Jumbo's keeper may have seen to the elephant's bath before he slept, but definitely not his own. "Matthew Scott?"

He pushed in front of Jumbo and took hold of the playful trunk bound for Nell. "Scotty'll do…miss. And Jumbo doesn't like strangers."

"Then he's in the worst possible place." She thought about offering her nicely cleaned gloved hand, then no. "I'm Nell Kelly. Little Nell Kelly. I'm the circus's star performer. Perhaps you've heard of me?"

From the gaunt gaze, the Englishman hadn't or was still too tired to care. Nell was determined to hate him as much as Jumbo. "Miss Kelly to you will do. And I've grown up around circus elephants. I'm to accompany Jumbo during the promenade each night with Tom Thumb. He's our little elephant, likes to run about the ring stealing cakes and getting chased by a clown. Mr. Barnum thinks he and I'll make Jumbo look even bigger. Just thought I'd come round this morning and say how do." Unexpectedly, Nell heard herself add, "He's not well, is he?"

Scotty was still wrestling with Jumbo's trunk. "I'd know if he wasn't."

"Of course you would. I'll see you, then, before my show." She turned with as much disdain as she could muster, just to let him know this was a fight she planned to win, and hoped he was getting a good look at her bustle.

"Wait. Why would you say that, about my Jumbo being sick?"

Glancing back, Nell shrugged and noticed that Matthew Scott, even filthy, wasn't so hard on the eyes. "Like I said...I've been around elephants."

"And why wasn't I told about you?"

"You're in the circus now."

Jumbo snorted and shifted at the man crunching sand hard under boot.

"Why, Miss Nell." Elephant Bill, bullhook in hand, pushed Scotty out of the way. Drove his iron into the ground by her feet. "Aren't you looking like a cake sweet enough to lick the frosting off this morning."

She closed her eyes against his hot, foul breath. No way was she going to show anyone how much Bill terrified her, made her shake, but the more she tried, the more she failed.

"That's my girl. And how's our big African brute this morning? You feed him, English?"

Scotty rubbed his hand down Jumbo's trunk. "Washed and eating well, now that the ground doesn't move and he's out of that box. A few more weeks' rest and I'll have him ready to try walking about that ring out there. Slow and steady, I'd say. Hippodrome, is it?"

Elephant Bill yanked his bullhook out of the sand, shoved Scotty aside. Stood face to face with Jumbo. Nell knew that look, felt queasy, was thankful she'd not eaten yet. *No Bill, don't! Please don't! You take one of the other girls tonight...* But Elephant Bill never changed his mind, not when it was set.

"You and me, English, we don't speak the same language. That'd be American, if you're wondering. I talk; you do as I say. Get the chains off and this animal into the ring."

"I'm Jumbo's keeper. I'll say when he's ready." Sounded as if Scotty was used to animals being wild, just not so smart about men being that way. "He's been boxed into that crate for weeks and I say he needs rest."

Bill tossed his hook onto the straw-strewn floor. "Get along, Nell, nothing for you to see here," and grabbed Scotty by his shirt. Got real close. Behind them, Jumbo shifted about noisily, a long, warning draught of air snorted through his trunk.

"I'll take this up with Mr. Barnum—"

"You don't see Mr. Barnum. You see me. And you don't want me to be the last person you ever see." Bill tightened his grip on Scotty. "Now you listen to me, English. You fucked me around for weeks in London, mincing about with your secret hand signs—*Jumbo do this, Jumbo do that*—getting folks riled about this elephant leaving, and me spit on. Acting like you ruled the roost. Yeah, I knew what you were doing. We all did. Bartlett warned me. Your boss couldn't wait to see the backside of you. All those times Jumbo didn't go into that box—because of you. Missed all those ships, cost Mr. Barnum a lot of money. But I says, Bill, hold your tongue. Day'll come."

To Scotty's credit, he met stare with stare. But by the sound of that leg chain getting yanked, Nell figured Jumbo'd had enough.

"And you know why I did that? Because I needed your pansy arse to help me get that elephant right here. And English, I don't need you anymore. Every night, thousands are gonna pay to see these bastard elephants dance, and by Christ, this one will too. Me? I don't give a damn what the posters make him out to be. All I know is you're here just long enough to settle him in. Now, do we speak the same language, because it looks to me like you'd be understanding American pretty good right about now. If not, I'll toss your arse on the next steamer back to London, and it'll be just me and Jumbo here." Bill grabbed his hook from off the floor. "Get those leg irons off him."

Elephant Bill yelled loudly for Jumbo to follow, and when he didn't, thrust his hook into his backside. Jumbo roared and reared his head back, looked at Scotty.

Helpless, motionless with childlike impotence in the elephant's wake. His elephant. Quickly understanding all too well what the circus would be. Not the adversary Nell wanted to face.

"He'll learn to listen to me." This time Bill's bullhook skewered Jumbo's trunk, resulting in a painful howl.

Scotty ran to his side, patted Jumbo gently. "Please…stop… you're hurting him."

"This animal is no pet, English. Now grab your whip and help me break him. Or pack your bag."

Nell ignored Bill and followed, but she didn't know why. She sure didn't want to see what she knew was coming. Animals got hurt all the time, no different what Bill was doing now. Barnum's other elephants, they feared the spike at the top of his iron. Dead inside, jabs made them move. Took it, until they were too old. Or mistakenly fought back. But Jumbo? Why was she feeling different about this animal she'd vowed to hate? Him being here taking away everything she had! But the flash of fight, when hook pierced flesh, came out red—not like other animals. He was keeping score. She could see it in those eyes. She'd seen something like that before. In a mirror, after Bill…her waiting for the day when an account got settled. Only, when it came to Elephant Bill getting his comeuppance, it wouldn't be because of Jumbo.

NELL REMEMBERED EVERY DETAIL FROM HER FIRST TIME WITH Elephant Bill. She'd just come back from being celebrated, and chased, through Buckingham Palace. *Sensational Little Nell Kelly!* Bill's worn leather trousers smelled of horseshit, coarse black hair poked through his cotton shirt, mouth buried under an untrimmed moustache, and big ears sticking out from the sides of his head. Had more hair back then.

He shook a bag of saltwater taffy, asked why not come behind the camel tent. Have a taste. Smell of taffy can still make Nell throw up, just like that. Back then, taffy tasted sweet. Bill gave her so much candy her jaws kind of stuck together, mouth couldn't be used for yelling when he pinned her and slipped his fingers inside. Shush, shush, you little slut, he whispered, and that with some practice, she'd learn to love him poking around down there.

Bill had a mind to help himself to someone little like Nell, but they'd been too ugly until she came along. Wanted to see if they were like a real woman, responded like a real woman. Right beauty, he whispered about Nell in her ear when he took his tongue out. First time he shoved his prick into her, Nell bled so much she was light-headed for days. Tightest cunt he'd ever had. Squeezed the seed right out of him. Had his hand over her mouth, but it being so big, covered her nose too, so she almost passed out. He got better with practice.

Pretty easy from then on for Elephant Bill to get his way. Happened all the time. Nala gave her one of her hand-painted silk scarves by way of consolation and Zip avoided looking at her, humming a song about one more day to tote the weary load. Everyone knew better than to speak up. Clowns suddenly remembered a boot lace needing tying or a button needing sewing so as to miss when one of the men had a girl by the hand and was dragging her off behind a tent. If they got sick, girls'd just be gone before their bellies showed. Always off to visit a grandmother or take care of a sick relative. Never left a way of getting a letter to them. Never came back. While no one ever talked about it, looking after yourself was best learned early.

Nell's mistake was thinking Bill was done with her, and Dora was just being kind to her friend after she'd moved out of her private railcar for Jumbo. *So nice to have you back with us, Nell. Take the bottom bunk, Nell, on account of you being such a big star.* Not the first time Elephant Bill had come sniffing around the clown car. He didn't like climbing up to the top bunks in case he rolled off when he got to grunting. Dora'd heard all right. Everyone had. They just pulled the curtains by their bunks and shoved bits of cotton in their ears. Nell screamed until she figured out Bill liked that even more. After, Dora climbed down and rubbed her back and let her cry. Gave Nell a salve and a bottle of amber. Wash yourself out, she said, because no one wanted a bastard from that bastard.

Nell did try telling Bill she was going to Mr. Barnum. He'd never let Bill get away with taking liberties with his famous Little Eyes Nell. Bill laughed. Said go ahead, so she did. The circus was outside of Baltimore, and Mr. Barnum's private railcar was parked on a siding. She tried to get in several times, and each time Mr. Bailey shooed her away, told to come back later, Mr. Barnum was very busy. So, she waited until no one was about and the car was empty. The splendour inside almost made Nell forget why she'd come. Sofas and chairs upholstered in regal blue, engraved nameplate on the carved mahogany desk, carpets patterned in shades of paprika, walls of cushioned leather, and crystal gas globes. But she hid in the water closet—basins of white porcelain and a handle that, when pulled, flushed unmentionables away. She hated to think about Mr. Barnum using it, but it was a long wait and she used it just the same.

When he came through the door and found Nell waiting, the old man didn't get a chance to even be surprised. She blurted everything Elephant Bill was doing to her, no breaths in between, afraid if she stopped and looked into the man's face, she'd see what she feared the most—her confession doing more harm than good. At some point during her lament, Barnum eased down onto the exquisite blue sofa, hands between his knees, and stared at the paprika flooring. When she was done, he leaned back, pulled an embroidered handkerchief from his pocket, and wiped his forehead.

"My dear Nell." He shook his head wearily. "Why is it you little people always tell the biggest lies? And about a God-fearing man like our Bill? A family man. A good man. A religious man."

Had she spoken in a language he couldn't understand? "Mr. Barnum—"

"I'm not deaf to your plight, dear Nell. You still mean a great deal to me and this circus and those who pay to see you. In spite of these…hurtful fancies of yours."

Her smile on the side of a train used to be the first glimpse of the circus. Now she meant nothing. The monster got away with the deed, and Nell, humbled, awaited judgment.

"I must pray on this matter. Yes, pray. Do you pray to the Lord, Little Eyes?" The old man stood, unsteady. Footsteps outside meant others were coming. "I shall give thanks my circus has an army of elephants needing keeping, and Bill is the man to do it. And I'll pray that I don't need to find someone else to fit your costumes. Now, run along and get ready for the show."

She pushed her way through young men tumbling into the coach. The empty glare of afternoon waited outside.

"You all right there, Nell?" saluted one of the circus lads walking by as she climbed down the steps from the railcar.

She raised her hand against the sun. "It's never going to stop." *I'm nothing more than an animal, a disposable animal. No better than Jumbo.*

"What's that you say?"

"Never…stop…"

"Right-o," said the young man, with a wave and a smile. Trumpets started tuning in the distance.

Every time Elephant Bill climbed on top of Nell after that, and she felt his stinking breath on her neck, his tongue in her ear, hot wet black tobacco juice dripping down her cheek, pushed down her shoulders as he arched his back and screamed ah ah sweet Jesus before he shot into her, she stayed right there in her head. Didn't go off, imagining posies in a garden or what it'd be like to wriggle her toes in beach sand trying to forget. Nell wanted to remember every thrust, every stink, every grunt, and who she needed to get even with.

NELL FOLLOWED SCOTTY ON THAT FIRST MORNING TOUR, Elephant Bill jabbing at Jumbo—"That's it, keep moving, you giant lazy beast; see, he'll soon mind me"—while he pointed out the Hippodrome, hundreds of feet long, circling three central rings surrounded by banks of seats. Tenting was fixed to the curved iron framework overhead, wired with those newfangled electrics, so that at night the Greatest Show on Earth was harshly, hotly, and dazzlingly illuminated.

Watching Jumbo miserably prodded about on the end of that man's unrelenting bullhook, Nell didn't think Scotty heard a word.

"Mr. Barnum shows his oddities and curiosities in that ring." Bill winked at Nell. "Got one for the big cats, tumblers and trapeze in another. And all around, could be a parade of elephants. Crowd goes wild when they see them all lined up, trumpeting. Mr. Barnum's got hundreds of horses and trick riders, zebras, giraffes. Sometimes we even get up a chariot race like those old Romans did. Or we just march all around with the bands playing. Can't hear yourself think. Mr. Barnum's got women that can dance the dead out of their graves, or make a man glad to be alive—but don't bother sniffing around, they're poxy—and more clowns than you can count. Damn thieving bastards—so hands in your pockets." He rammed his hook into Jumbo, snarling Jumbo, Scotty flinching at every blow, trailing his whip in the sand. "Dreams, English, dreams. That's what Mr. Barnum gives every man, woman, and child who pays the admission."

To Nell, having your life explained by the somebody running it always made it sound better than it was.

THE PEACOCK DRESS

Madison Square Garden, 1882

On the day the *New York Tribune* ran the headline "English Elephant Runs Amok, Nearly Kills Beloved Circus Performer," Barnum hosted a luncheon at Delmonico's on Fifth Avenue for Mayor Grace, where he announced the date of Jumbo's first circus appearance. The mayor's wife fanned herself to a frenzy when hearing about poor little Nell's near demise. Her concern, however, did not extend to talking *to* Nell, who attended the luncheon with Barnum, paraded much like a dog on a leash. But Mrs. Grace *must* have tickets to see Jumbo just the same. Then Barnum magnanimously offered, to much applause, free entry for the city's foundlings. Why should being disadvantaged deprive the wee ones of the opportunity to see the spoils of war for themselves?

The orphans never came. Instead, hundreds of gold-coloured tickets granting the bearer free admission to the premiere were carried in a leather pouch by self-aggrandized balloonist Professor Donaldson, who, having given up his quest to float across the Atlantic, drifted upwards in Barnum's service once or twice a week from Madison Square Garden in a hot air balloon festooned with painted garlands of roses and camelias. Over 40th Street, he tossed the gold tickets overboard. The cards were weighted at one end and, as they fell, twirled like maple keys, falling through plate glass shattered by milk cans thrown off the back of overturned wagons and spinning wheels of collided carriages, their drivers having dropped reins to grab at the prize. The melee caused two broken arms, a dislocated shoulder, and a surprising number of torn women's skirts.

None of this buffoonery was inadvertent, as Nell well knew. The closest Jumbo came to running amok, or running anywhere, was when he plucked a gardenia out of her hat as Scotty walked him around the Hippodrome, then spit it out when he realized it was made of silk. When it came to selling tickets, few were better than Barnum. In a city already crowded with delights, his circus was an event not to be missed. Outright lying to the press, if you please, but that was something Nell knew the showman was too much of a Christian to admit. Besides, was there really a sin when the result brought joy into miserable lives? Surly obfuscation could be God's work. But you'd think with those stories, nobody'd feel safe coming to see Jumbo. Already, that lineup for tickets was around the block. Fastest time a season's ever been sold out, Nell heard Mr. Hutchinson happily say, even figuring the first fifty folks waiting were paid to stand in line, just to get people fearing they'd miss out.

Still, the thought of that elephant going berserk did have appeal for Nell. She hated to admit it, but that fool Dora was putting words to Nell's worry. Lots of attention was being made over an elephant—imagine!—and where would that leave her? Anyone who could fit into her costumes could take her place. Best thing that could happen now was for Jumbo to go on a rampage—not a big one, just enough to knock about a few bleachers, maybe a pole or two, even a few bruises—get Mr. Barnum to realize Jumbo was too dangerous to be parading about the Hippodrome in front of so many people. And, Lord love us, children! But Nell didn't bother to tell Scotty about men with rifles at the ready in case Jumbo did act up. She'd learned that from Elephant Bill one of those times he'd crawled into her bunk. Guess he thought her knowing he could kill the beast might put her at ease walking beside Jumbo every night.

Scotty had a handful of days to get Jumbo ready for the show. He scrubbed up well, Scotty that is, for a man so clearly not used to it. Black woollen coat with tails, crisp linen shirt, and white bow tie—even if he did say it felt like wearing someone else's hot skin—for which he now had to shave and trim his moustache. The top hat he liked to see himself wearing in the mirror.

"I feel like the Earl of Derby." Scotty's face then darkened as if the comparison was a grievous sin.

If Scotty could be so finely turned out for the grand event, then, Nell insisted, so must she. All this money and effort being spent on Jumbo's big night, and wouldn't that reflect poorly on Mr. Barnum, his other great performer shabby as a milkmaid in some old threadbare dress she'd worn hundreds of times? Why, shouldn't Nell look the part too? She'd be walking right beside an elephant costing more money than working folks saw in five lifetimes. Best look like it.

"Quite right, Little Eyes. I'll leave the details to you. You know best what you little folks need. But make it spectacular."

Oh, she intended to. What Nell had in mind, no one would be looking at Jumbo. And when Barnum saw all those people calling her name, he'd have to put that elephant back in the box. Jumbo and Scotty. Though she was starting to feel sorry for Scotty. Not much of a talker. Fish out of water, for sure, but not once did he look at Nell like she was something to be afraid of. His breath stunk of an alehouse, but she figured Scotty needed something to dull the ache of Elephant Bill, who was now forcing him to use his bullhook and whip on Jumbo. Zoo animals in England must have got treated differently. Maybe it was some quaint English custom to rinse your mouth with cheap rosewater to hide the drink. It wasn't working, and Nell thought she should tell him don't bother, everyone in the circus drinks. Of course, Barnum forbid it, but it was more a case of forbidding himself to know about the grease that kept the circus running.

THE BROWNSTONE WAS BELOW HOUSTON STREET, HAD NO MARquee, impenetrable green blinds obscured the windows, and was whispered to be the one shop in New York City where men came who liked to dress as women, no questions asked. And the most expensive.

The tiled entrance was unadorned and the well-tailored, profusely perfumed man behind the counter, whose facial hair resembled an intricately manicured parterre, gave no indication that the ringing bell announcing Nell's entrance was anything usual.

"I'm here to see Montmorency."

The Book, as it was known, was retrieved from a drawer and a finger sliding down a ledger confirmed Nell's appointment. The man bowed slightly, led her to the double doors, and with both hands on the crystal knobs, threw them open so that Nell got the full effect.

"Oh my!"

Black-and-white-striped fabric was draped from the ceiling and walls, tent-like over a splashing fountain, sandalwood incense smoked from burners under brass chimes, and leather ottomans trimmed in gold fringe dotted overlaying Persian carpets. A caravanserai plucked from the road to Kabul.

"Come back in two months," said the gatekeeper without expression, "and he will have changed it all."

Meaning Montmorency. A slight man with a thin moustache that looked pencilled, tightly fitted in black with a cravat of grey and silver. His greeting was effusive. Delight was expressed by holding his hands together as if in prayer, and lightly clapping. The sort of man whom you'd expect to pepper every sentence with an affected *bon mots, en Français,* just to remind you he's better, but who surprisingly had a deep voice with a Southern accent. But to Nell, his feet, tiny for a man, were divine, sheathed as they were in shoes of pointed red leather.

Nell was then taken through a flap in the tent. Other men, similar in style to Montmorency but in various degrees of size and age, darted in and out of doors carrying bolts of fabric, ribbons, and intricate drawings as if on their way to a military campaign. In a private room where mirrors and lacquer panels of men and women in kimonos cupping lotus blossoms covered the walls, the dressmaker offered her a seat.

"Sweet Beulah, churn my butter!" he said when Nell showed him her roughly sketched idea.

"Can you do it? It must be ready quickly."

The man held up the paper and lightly traced her lines with his fingers.

"Never been done before."

"But can you do it?"

"Nell, honey, I can stitch a cow into taffeta." He slowly nodded his head, as if calculating. "For a price."

No matter, as far as Nell was concerned. By the time Barnum got Montmorency's bill, she'd once again be the circus's biggest attraction.

MAGIC AND SLEIGHT OF HAND DO NOT COME EASY, AND THE DAY OF Jumbo's debut in the Greatest Show on Earth began even earlier than most. Performers needed to brush coats and trousers and, with delicate needlework, darn and stitch glass beads to costumes, boots and buttons rubbed until sparkling. Hundreds of mewling and growling animals needed food and water, manes braided, harnesses polished. Seating swept and more benches added wherever they could be fitted. *Tickets! Tickets! Tickets!* Everyone in New York was begging, borrowing, or stealing for the much-sought-after entry. Horns shined; strings tuned. Drums tested. Oil lamps filled and great cloth curtains pulled.

Scotty'd been fussing with his costume all morning. Coat on, coat off. Hat on, hat off. Could Miss Nell help him with his bow tie, she could stand on that empty crate to do so. Nell caught him tippling from a flask. Serve him right, then, if Jumbo bolted and he too drunk to do anything. Sure as eggs is eggs, they'd both be on a ship back to England. Good. But on second thought, Nell would be standing right beside Jumbo, and if he rampaged, likely it'd be her he stepped on. Probably wouldn't live through that. And there were those men of Elephant Bill's with rifles, maybe with not so good aim. She sighed deeply. Only wanted Jumbo gone, not dead.

"Who's Mr. Vanderbilt?" Scotty asked.

"Richest man in New York, folks say." Nell nervously helped herself to the offered flask from Scotty. All the performances she'd been through and tonight she had butterflies. "But if you ask me, rich folks always say they're the richest. Mr. Barnum says this one owns the Hippodrome. Probably a guest of honour."

Standing beside Jumbo, waiting for their moment, she pulled the draped black cotton cloak about her tightly. Neck to ground. Only thing that gave away her costume underneath were the towering ostrich feathers in her cap. Jumbo kept sniffing about her, tugging at the cloak.

"Mr. Scott, if you please! I've told Jumbo he doesn't see it before anyone else."

Outside in the Hippodrome, voices swelled. Boots and shoes scuffed along rough planking, wood creaking as people took seats, chatted excitedly, waved to friends, and tittered nervously, expectantly. As one by one the gas lamps glowed, and the electrics buzzed, the colour drained from Scotty's face.

"You'll be fine, Mr. Scott. Jumbo too." Or maybe not, hoped Nell.

Of all of them, the star of the show was the least bothered by the growing din coming from the rings. Jumbo, legs clinking in heavy irons, shuffled and swayed behind his curtain, Nell by his side, Scotty in tow with his whip and bullhook. Nell was glad for the occasional flap of the animal's ears, air moving in their confinement a welcome respite from her dreadfully heavy gown. Almost as if he knew that she was agitated, Jumbo wrapped his trunk about her arm. Nell was about to shrug him off and Scotty, stepping forward, No Jumbo, no, but Nell unexpectantly felt her racing heart slow and, pleasantly relieved, nodded Scotty back to his place. Soon, this would all be over.

Broken applause and laughter meant the start of the preliminary amusements—ostriches ridden by stuffed monkeys, running round the outside track—as the last of the audience squeezed into tight spaces. The recreation of an English hunt followed, with hounds and lords and ladies in hunting jackets—although the fox immediately bolted out of the sandy ring and through an open door, preferring to take its chances dodging wheels and wagons on the streets of Manhattan. Then a steeplechase, round and round, until banging drums and trumpets signalled performers to clear the Hippodrome.

After a suitably dramatic pause, the slow march of Barnum's Congress of Nations. Nell had witnessed the procession a hundred times but tonight, even to her, it felt unexpectedly fresh and thrilling. Not nations of the modern world, but ancient Egypt and Greece and Rome. Gods and goddesses. Magnificent stallions and brawny, half-naked men painted brown and carrying standards and torches, and litters of scantily clad women eating and tossing fruit from platters while horrified mothers in the stands covered the eyes of their boys. And men. Then paraded Russian czars with false beards and English kings—Henry VIII carrying a papier mâché head of Anne Boleyn—Chinese emperors escorted by black chow chows panting blue tongues, and Spain's Isabella and Ferdinand sending Columbus off to discover the New World. A band marched into the centre ring, keeping all stepping in time around the outer Hippodrome. No matter where you sat, a spectacle to delight.

In the far-left ring, men and women, even children, wearing sky blue tights suddenly descended from the high wires and began swinging and flipping. A collective gasp as snapping lions were chased in underneath to the crack of whips. In the far-right ring, a woman with fiery hair named Skye of the Highlands galloped in on a horse and shot at bottles rotating on a round dais in the centre.

When the last of the Congress of Nations waved their farewell, the parade of animals began. Antelopes and gazelles, pacing and snarling tigers rolled in cages, donkeys, stately plodding giraffes, trick-horse riders racing in and about, somersaulting on and off their mounts, shooting into the gasping audience with rifles that only fired confetti. Hercules replaced Skye the redheaded horsewoman. A polar bear rolled on its back under the trapeze artists. Clowns tumbled about with horns and drums, making a great show of getting in everyone's way until chariots manned with shouting centurions raced in and cleared their outer ring for the games. Alongside them, a covered wagon, a pioneer man and woman equally determined. A race of ages to the death, around the Hippodrome to horns and cheers so loud Nell had to cover her ears and she was sure that no one in the stands could hear Jumbo anxiously trumpet. The end was abrupt, and a gasp cut short the cheering crowd. Nell had no wish to know who had won, for surely some animal had lost.

Wagons covered with bunting and filled with musicians, brassy and banging of drums, accompanied the entrance of the slow, lumbering elephant parade, led by Bill—yaw! yaw!—in a red velvet coat, expertly snapping whips from both hands. Barnum had so many elephants that when Tom Thumb, the miniature elephant named after the showman's once famous performer, entered the Hippodrome, the animals encircled the perimeter with barely a breath between them.

The three centre rings filled with banner-draped horn players, heralding the main event so loudly Nell was sure even the dead of New York City must have heard. Then silence. So too the thousands crammed in tiered seats about the three rings, the outer track. Air hot, nervous coughs, added to the potent stink of animal shit, sweat, stale tobacco, and smoking kerosene.

Then, stomping feet.

Clapping hands.

Give us Jumbo!

Louder.

Bring out Jumbo!

The drums began a slow pounding and Elephant Bill, theatrically flaying his whips, forced all animals to turn inward to face the curtain shielding Jumbo. The two outer rings emptied, then quickly filled with Barnum's menagerie of African bounty: zebras, camels, ostriches, horses, dogs, giraffes, sword- and staff-bearing warriors and maidens from the Congress of Nations. At the cessation of the drums, all who could kneel paid homage with the clinking and rattling of necklaces and armbands and armour. After another rapid beat of the drums and Elephant Bill snapping whips, all the elephants went down on their front legs.

The roar of the audience was deafening. Surely those outside Madison Square Garden must be stopped in wonder. Nell glanced back at Scotty, who was miserably draining his flask.

"Be ready," she hissed.

The clapping and cheering continued long and loud, then slowly trailed off, the audience realizing nothing would happen until there was silence. And when that moment came, the curtain in front of them was slowly parted. Jumbo prodded, stepped into the ring, Nell dropped her black cloak behind her and, hand against his rough and creased side, marched into the centre ring alongside him, Scotty so dazzled and distracted by the pageantry that Elephant Bill strode in ready behind him.

In later shows, Nell might promenade. Sometimes she'd sing "Oh! Dem Golden Slippers!" or "Why Did They Dig Ma's Grave So Deep?" Tom Thumb might squeak and scamper about them in playful circles. Scotty at ease by then, striding about like an earl. On Jumbo's back, his old *London Zoo* howdah crawling with kids. Except no one noticed that they weren't children at all. Mr. Hutchinson was dead set against that. Couldn't have real young'uns getting tossed and trampled if Jumbo went African—as Elephant Bill liked to say. So, any performer who could pass muster dressed as a child climbed on Jumbo's back with strict orders to watch their cussing and spitting before the audience.

But not tonight, not this first of so many spectacular nights.

Nell grinned, laughed a little even, confident she would steal Jumbo's thunder. Take some pleasure in ruining Barnum's evening. Her exquisite Peacock Dress, fitted bodice, her tightly corseted waist pulled into a V, the envy of every woman that night. And women got men to buy tickets. Paisley from breast to toe swirled with the colours of South Seas aquamarine and turquoise, lime and olive and leafy forest greens, sparkling desert sand, and orange-red equatorial sunsets, delicately embroidered with gold and silver thread and peacock feathers. Montmorency told her, along with giving her the bill, nothing he'd created before, and surely nothing he'd create after, would ever eclipse this achievement. The dress appeared to shimmer with iridescent colours, but when Jumbo and Nell made their way with church-like silence to centre ring, she held out her arms for one final delight. The cloth bands attached to her wrists pulled up the cape behind her, a cape inlaid with set pieces of stained glass. The effect being that as Nell walked beside Jumbo, the lights of the Hippodrome reflected a moving kaleidoscope on Jumbo's hide. On cue, he glanced back at his keeper, lifted his head, and trumpeted wildly.

Applause erupted, cheers and whistles, as one by one the audience jumped up, until thousands were screaming, *Jumbo! Jumbo!* Men who'd spent a week's wages on a single ticket. Downtrodden women in made-over dresses breathlessly glimpsing an exotic world where someone else cooked dinner and babies didn't come every year. Children who, as old men and women, would regale grandchildren in awed tones about the day they saw Jumbo. The Great Jumbo. Here, this night in Madison Square Garden, Barnum's Roman Hippodrome, where even the Vanderbilts, hobnobbing in silks and muslins, bored easily from a life of privilege, danced to the organ grinder that was Barnum.

But Nell only felt the weight of the Peacock Dress and its failure. Yes, these people cheered, they adored...not her, but an elephant puffed up in humbug and lies. One of dozens already before him. How could P. T. Barnum have created such a sensation? An animal with broken tusks and a foul temper, a half-drunk keeper in tow. Rage and rampage now, she thought, let this fool audience and their misguided devotion see Scotty fall over in his drink, Elephant Bill ordering rifle fire from the sidelines. She'd not give one damn. Because they weren't cheering for her, seeing her, reminding Barnum how special she was, and not like...Bucephalus. Poor, dear

Bucephalus. Not that fate. Only the bullet to her head wouldn't be swift. Bill would see to that.

Her steps faltered under the weight of the dress she now thought absurd, the gown she'd take off, box up, and hide, say it was stolen, and never wear again. No one noticed. No one cared. Except the sand beneath her feet, slowly rising to cushion her fall, and wondering how it would feel against her cheek, when the gentle squeezing about her arm held her up. Jumbo's trunk, and his large, moist eyes upon her. All she could think of in that uplifting moment, a moment that Scotty would drunkenly recount over and over—He pulled you right back up, miss!—was the anguish on the face of that woman she'd rescued from a burning church. How the look in those painted eyes haunted Nell, as if she would come to understand why.

WESTWARD HO, ELEPHANT!

Hudson River, 1882

Partial victory or magnanimous defeat, Nell wasn't sure, but in those days following Jumbo's triumphant spring debut she found herself pulled uncomfortably in directions she hadn't anticipated. Jumbo hadn't destroyed the Hippodrome, run wildly into the spectator seats, or even knocked over a barrel of water. Good as gold, if anything. Ticket sales made him the undisputed luminary of the moment. And while her name no longer appeared on the posters, Nell convinced herself she was sharing the top billing by his side. At least there'd been no further talk about finding someone else to wear her costumes.

To Dora, who'd come round saying that Elephant Bill was mighty put out about Nell not seeing to his affections, she said Bill knew where to find her: tucked in at night beside Jumbo. While Bill feared no animal, he wasn't stupid enough to drag Nell kicking and screaming from under an elephant with a temper. Not that the arrangement was bound to cause any scandal. Scotty's only got eyes for that elephant, Dora said, and everyone could see that. Every so often the circus came across those sorts of men, men of few words, not partial to others. Certainly not women. Except when Scotty talked with Jumbo. Such endearments, sweetly spoken. To Nell overhearing them, it was like ice melting on the tongue for the first time. A fleeting wonder, wanting more. And for men like Scotty, that kind of attachment never ended well.

The only bee in the butter was his drinking. Maybe the English drank more, although hard to imagine. Nell knew horsemen who drank ale all day and still managed hoop jumps in the evening show. Scotty, and Jumbo, was way beyond even a tankard of ale so it was with a tinge of conscience that she eagerly filled Scotty's teacup from her milk bottle, painted white to evade the temperance edicts of the God-fearing Mr. Barnum. Drink, as the showman was fond to preach, was the key to perdition. Maybe so, but the offer of whiskey was the only way for Nell to wrest substance from a man of so few words or allow her to follow him to the animal pens after the performance.

"I do believe he's getting the way of the circus. Quick learner, my Jumbo," Scotty said, tossing back the last of his *tea*. For the first time since he'd arrived in New York, the man sounded like his world might be turning in the right direction.

He and Nell sat in Jumbo's shadow; the steady crunch of cabbage being fed into his mouth.

"I've been thinking, Mr. Scott, when I walk out there with Jumbo, if I touch him, his skin feels, I don't know...loose. Is that normal? You think he's eating enough?" Surprised Nell to hear herself caring.

"Rubbish. If anyone knew Jumbo was poorly, that'd be me. You don't know what it was like in that ship's hold, waves washing over us, rats, the bloody rats. All of us being...in a mighty off way because of the waves. And Bill forcing him out there when he's not been properly rested."

Nell reached down to unbutton her shoes. "But he doesn't smell right. Been around lots of sick animals, and they got a smell to 'em when they're poorly inside."

"Ah, you sound like Lux-Bourquet. Doctor dressed prettier than a woman. The Society paid that damn Belgian fool too much money if you ask me, just to make sure Jumbo was healthy enough to sell. Could have told them that. Said his molars weren't growing right. Hurt when he ate, and if an animal the size of Jumbo stops eating, the end's quick. And me by Jumbo's side for twenty years. Wouldn't I know?"

Felt good to kick off the shoes. "Maybe he's homesick."

"Now that's something you are right about, Miss Nell. But we'll soon fix that." Scotty helped himself to Nell's milk bottle. "Six months. That's how long Bartlett said he'd hold a place for me. People'll be tired of looking at Jumbo long before then. Mr. Barnum too. Won't be able to send us home fast enough. You'll see."

Of all the outcomes, this was one Nell hadn't considered, nor, in all honesty, thought probable. "The London Zoo will take Jumbo back?"

"Ha! What nonsense, Nell." The familiarity was always a presage to rip-snorting sleep. "I'm talking *Jumbo*'s home. Sudan, where those hunters took him from his mother. He remembers. I made a promise...a river...to take him back."

The liquor did its job. The porcelain cup tumbled out of Scotty's hand.

NELL DIDN'T EXPECT TO FIND HERSELF LOOKING FORWARD TO those moments before she led Jumbo into the Hippodrome under hot lights, cheers and applause and crashing music, trick ponies and barking dogs and clowns in garish greasepaint, Scotty fussing with buttons or his tie. The world's tiniest woman and its largest elephant, side by side, her hand pressed against rough, grey skin, feeling his giant beating heart. Nell promised herself never to care for an animal, not after Bucephalus, and especially not Jumbo. She'd close her eyes, listening to the gentle flap of Jumbo's ears, his snorts of anticipation, like a prayer stamping everything else quiet, feel the *bump bump* underneath as his feet shifted about on the sand. Crush her in an instant and yet, she had no fear. Sometimes even, being silly, she'd think Jumbo made a better God than the one up there who was hard of hearing. Then slowly, the cheers out there in the Hippodrome and the drums and horns and tambourines a reminder her dreams were not her own.

"Miss Nell, if you please, how do I look?" Scotty, fussing like a schoolboy.

That fancy suit he'd first bristled under had become a source of pride. Buttons had to be polished. Fabric brushed. Collar turned. He'd hold his arms out and present himself for inspection. After all, folks out there paid to see Jumbo, but they knew Scotty. You could see the man puff with pride as he led the elephant around the Hippodrome. *Jumbo! Mr. Scott!* In London he mucked out stalls, but here in New York City, he was Mr. Scott, Jumbo's keeper.

"A walk around the ring twice a day. Not a bad life is this," he'd say to Nell, Jumbo eased back into his pen, never having seen the sun or the clouds or felt rain or wondered if birds in America were different than in London, irons being snapped about his leg. "And look, Jumbo likes it too. He's getting fat. And you being worried."

But Scotty didn't believe a sunny word about Jumbo coming out of his own mouth, although he tried, and Nell could tell. She served *tea*. More each night. A bottle for Jumbo too. His appetite for it, she learned, prodigious from his days at the zoo.

Jumbo's hide hung on him; he was listless. If Scotty thought he ate well, it was because Elephant Bill kept him on half rations. Starving elephants were docile. Jumbo wasn't allowed the companionship of his own kind and twice around the ring was nothing compared to crowded walks around the London Zoo petted by hundreds, his back burdened with those who could afford the penny ride. All this wearing in Scotty's face, creased and early old. If Scotty needed to drink himself to sleep each night, Nell was glad to oblige. Jumbo swaying back and forth, his trunk sniffing food barrels he'd already emptied, and Scotty soon to be snoring on his cot. No one paid any mind to Nell curling up in the nearby straw, the gentle tugging of chains soothing like waves.

"Just like that terrier used to come round Jumbo's pen at the zoo." Scotty, heavy lidded, soon to be dreaming. "Kept the rats off him..."

Elephant Bill found them before dawn, forearms crossed against his beefy chest. No one had seen him for days, but there was talk about a wild gorilla named King Mykonos being purchased. Come from the Congo River, mean as thunder and no keeper up to the task of breaking him. But Elephant Bill was trying.

"Make Jumbo ready for the train." If he was surprised, or jealous, at seeing Nell in the straw, he was good at hiding it. "We march to the river."

Leave New York?

To Philadelphia, then Baltimore and Washington. Lots of one-saloon-three-church towns in between. After that, west to Cincinnati. Mostly, a matinee and evening show, then pack up and back on the rails. Might do a couple of days in, say, a place as big as Chicago, but takes some getting used to the stink from their slaughterhouses. Ride the train into southern Canada about the end of the summer before the snow comes, because that place is cold as hell half the year.

Scotty couldn't find words. Nell felt bad for him, the news being a shock she might have softened. But that was Scotty for you. Performers, animal trainers running around packing things up, glued-up posters announcing the summer tour, and he's thinking a cakewalk matinee and evening show in New York is never going to end.

The change of venue suited Bill just fine.

"So, English, bosses won't be watching over you on the road. That'll be me. I look forward to making sure Mr. Barnum wrings out every nickel, and then some, from his investment. Right, Jumbo?"

He slapped the elephant's thick skin.

"And Miss Nell, hate for Mr. Barnum to hear you not behaving like a good Christian woman."

LEAVING NEW YORK WAS SUPPOSED TO BE A QUIET AFFAIR, BUT NELL knew Barnum never missed a chance to toot his own horn. Half-page notices filled newspapers, ensuring crowds lined the route to the ferry, cheering, waving, getting free glimpses of Jumbo and never forgetting P. T. Barnum was the conjuror of marvels.

Elephant Bill ordered Scotty to hobble Jumbo's hind legs with heavier chains. No chance he was running loose during the walk from Madison Square Garden if he got spooked.

"Where you been, Miss Queen of Sheba?" asked Dora, siding up beside Nell and pulling her hand. "You taking up with that foreigner? Everyone says you are."

Nell freed herself. "I got nothing to say to you."

"You listen to me, Nell, if it's my bunk Bill fixes to crawl into because you're bedding down with that pigeon-livered wagtail, I'll be more than gobbing into your tea!"

Jumbo swung his head and gave Dora a wet snort with his trunk. Sent her on her way cursing and wiping. Like he knew when Nell needed someone being pushed off. Shielding her from those boys chucking rotten potatoes gone soft from rooftops and windowsills, damn near causing a stampede in those winding, tenement-lined streets, hussies in the windows tossing kisses and waving handkerchiefs. Even getting rid of worries about Bill. Walking alongside Jumbo's slow-stepping shadow made her think of nothing else but those great feet coming down, one after the other, believing there was some good reason for keeping your mouth shut when all you wanted to do was stop feeling bad for wishing him gone.

At the ferry landing, Elephant Bill circled around on his horse, reminded everyone he was the general in charge and wanted to save Mr. Barnum a few dollars by packing the paddlewheeler across the Hudson River to the New Jersey rail yards, so step lively.

Nell clung to a rope around Tom Thumb's neck, stood fixed beside Jumbo who was squawking and grunting, slowly getting pushed near the edge of the wobbly deck, so many elephants and camels and horses packed in tight behind him.

"Miss Nell, you'll be safer up here." Scotty hoisted her up on Tom's back as if she had no say about a man putting his hands on her. Hopefully having the wee elephant near Jumbo would calm him, especially if he spooked when the paddlewheels *swish-swish-swished*.

Mid-river, that's what happened.

Jumbo reared, the ferry tipped, and the paddlewheels rose out of the water, spinning and dripping. Elephant Bill was too far away on his horse to help Scotty stop Jumbo rocking the ferry, too many baying and squawking animals in between to hear what he was hollering.

That's when the elephants in behind Jumbo pushed in, pressed their heads against him like they were petting him with their trunks. Jumbo stopped his antics. The paddlewheels slowly set back into the water and Nell vowed, next time, she was swimming.

NELL'S OLD RAILCAR, PROPERTY OF BARNUM, BAILEY & HUTCHINSON, Sole Owners, was painted in red and blue, trimmed in gold: *Jumbo's Palace Car*. She told herself no angry tears at seeing her former home, but they came. The roof was raised so Jumbo could barely stand. Inside, table and chair in an alcove for Scotty, separated by a plank wall. Nell bounced on the cot, looked at the toilet with sadness and envy, peeved at it never being there when the railcar was hers.

Jumbo balked.

"He remembers." Reinforced walls, iron rings in the floor, chains dangling from the ceiling "Too much like that shipping crate." Scotty yanked on his walking stick wound up in Jumbo's trunk, like he was trying to drag him up the ramp, or Jumbo dragging Scotty out.

Elephant Bill set about ordering ropes and men, but Nell gingerly coaxed Jumbo inside the Palace railcar with an armful of apples.

"It'll do." Not much more than a glance, Scotty more concerned about Jumbo's comfort than his own. And in a moving railcar, he couldn't fathom how that could be.

Food would help settle the elephant, maybe a bottle or two.

"Doesn't like being on a train. Not one bit."

"Too bad we couldn't have Tom in here, that'd quiet him." Nell was looking under, looking over, seeing how she'd make herself fit right in.

"Where's your place?"

The ramp outside was being dragged off.

"Looks like I'll have to stay with you and Jumbo."

Scotty stabbed at the straw with a pitchfork while Nell rubbed Jumbo's trunk.

"When was that? Jumbo on a train."

"Near twenty years now. Jumbo just a calf. Superintendent sent me to bring him from Paris."

"Oh, Paris! Really, Mr. Scott?"

"Figured Jumbo was four or five years old then."

Only the second time Scotty'd been on a train. Lots of years in between not making him warm up to the experience. Lungs taking in black engine smoke, cinders in your eyes. Don't know why he was even sent, Thompson being the more senior keeper at the zoo. But he had two elephants to take care of, Jenny and Peter, and the other keeper good enough with big animals, Godfrey, was licking his lips at the idea of going to Paris with 450 pounds of the Society's money in his pocket. Probably why Superintendent Bartlett wasn't letting him out of his sight. Said Scotty was just the man to bring back the calf purchased from the Jardin des Plantes. Only African elephant in all of England.

"Sounds like a lot of money for an elephant."

"And one damn near dead."

"Do get to the Paris part, Mr. Scott."

What Scotty did see, he didn't much care for. Women smelling of lavender enough to make eyes water, pouring steaming milk in their sidewalk café coffee, carrying yappy dogs instead of letting them walk on the ground. Everyone too snooty and talking too fast to remember, but he knew well enough those Frenchies once cut off their queen's head and tossed it between her legs—even if it did happen a long time ago and sounds like she had it coming. Men with shiny hair and waistcoats dripping with silver, prettier than those women Godfrey warned him about with winks and elbow jabs. Red on their cheeks, show their ankles for a ha'penny. Pretty as you please, up and down those avenues, glancing at Scotty like he was dog shite standing there with everything he owned in a bag stitched from carpet. Anyhow, nice of that old man digging tulip bulbs by the gate to nod in the direction of the rotunda.

Scotty found Jumbo in there, no bigger than a mastiff, chained to a wall, the festering end of his trunk stretching for a rain puddle, swirling green after slowly moving through hippo shit. Scotty puked into a muck pile.

From the length of the chain, the farthest the baby elephant could move was about in his own filth. Eyes swollen shut, hide thick with scabs. Feet were the worst. French keeper blamed the rats. They came at night and the calf was too weak to fight them off. Flies swarmed during the day to suck on the open wounds. The Frenchman shook his head, threw his hands up, blamed it on the great Paris zoo buying everything a German trader named Hagenbeck offered just so London wouldn't get them, leaving no francs for feed. Other elephants made do with bellies full of sugar cakes and sweet rolls tossed with kisses for making children merry, and got fancy names like Castor and Pollux. That scrawny calf cowering in the dark was left to scratch timidly at scraps plucked from the mud.

Scotty jabbed the pitchfork hard into the bubble of Nell's Parisian fantasy. "Wanted to put my hands around that man's neck, but that'd not help wee Jumbo."

Up the track, the steam engine blasted a horn. Nell felt herself lurch as the wheels of her world slowly turned. Steaming elephant piss sloshed across the floor. Scotty would soon be drunk and scratching a bed for himself out of the hay. At least before Jumbo, when she was the celebrated Little Nell Kelly, in the fleeting razzle-dazzle between being sold and being devoured, she could imagine places like Paris as wonderful and waiting for her. But in the shadow of the world-famous Jumbo, in chains, a warning that being loved by thousands was only a vanity. Nell'd never be more than a freak carried through streets in a sack.

"Time has a way of making the thinking back on it not so bad," said Scotty. "But I'll tell you, that French keeper said Jumbo'd be dead before I got out of Paris. And when I got to London, Bartlett looked like I'd sold the cow for a handful of beans—even a simpleton would have left the diseased creature to its chances, which turned out to be none considering what happened when those Prussians invaded Paris. Expected I'd be sent home to Liverpool and have to take up brewing like my brother Tom. But I got Jumbo on a train to Calais, fed him the biggest sack of apples I could find. 'Course they went right through him, Jumbo not being used to food. But sure enough we crossed the channel, and then to London. Made him a promise: Don't die on me, I'll never leave your side."

BETWEEN A ROCK AND AN ELEPHANT

Jersey City, 1882

Dora couldn't wait to tell Nell that Camel Girl ran off, on account of Ella—that was Camel Girl's real name—nose in the air, always saying she was going to do better than her lot in the circus. She'd run off before—well, maybe not run exactly because her knees were backwards—so what kind of work was she going to get when people couldn't get past the staring? All freaks thought they'd do better, one time or another. Nell knew she'd be back.

"Mr. Bailey says you gotta take her place tonight, Nell." Dora was breathing hard as drama always left her short. "Sing a song or two. People miss hearing you sing."

Waiting to go on, Nell couldn't decide between "Paddy Duffy's Cart" and "Good Sweet Ham." Maybe she'd sing both. Dora was right. Hadn't been much singing since she'd taken up with Jumbo and Scotty. Audience was too busy cheering Jumbo to hear if she did. Not paying attention, that's when she felt the familiar hot stink puffing on her neck. Didn't even have to look to know.

"I got needs, Nell." Elephant Bill's promises to make up for lost time sounded like a growl. "And you can't hide by that elephant forever."

Like jumping awake from a nightmare, she had to tremble for a long time before she knew he was gone.

When it came to walking Jumbo around the ring under the big tent later that evening, he wouldn't let go, like he understood why Miss Nell kept looking behind her and why her heart was racing. Wrapped his trunk about Nell's arm, so nothing was getting between them. Never let go until they were inside the Palace railcar and the heavy wooden doors swung shut.

She helped Scotty pull off his fine coat, looking like he was going to pitch over into the hay. Drinking started early that day on account of the letter from London, but she couldn't blame him. He told her it was from that Superintendent Bartlett, and if Scotty wasn't coming back to the London Zoo after having those six months to get Jumbo settled, he could just as well enjoy nights on the rails, farm towns, smoky, lamp-lit, human stink–filled tents going up, tents going down, rocking railcars, hissing steam, all tucked in between a handful of smelly hours rolling between cornfields.

"Hutchinson says next year Mr. Barnum takes the circus to England." Scotty, swaying, slid back the railcar door, letting in the night. "Almost to Africa by then."

No point in Nell saying, most ideas come from Barnum were like smoke. Poof. Gone soon as they're formed.

Being too drunk to make the toilet, Scotty crawled in behind Jumbo. The stream of piss spraying off the boards was loud and steady. The circus train shunted onto a siding. Made Nell wonder how much help she'd need to tie someone like Elephant Bill to the tracks.

When the oncoming New York City passenger train hurled by, wheels grating and clacking, the noisy hot pinch of steam blasting through the open door terrified Jumbo, who shrieked, pulled, and fell back against the side of his den. Happened so fast, no time to cry out. Crunching sound Scotty made back there was like catching one of those June bugs between your fingers and squeezing.

DOZING IN THE KEROSENE-LIT CORNER BY THE SINK, DOC MURPHY'S head rolled onto his shoulder, wrapped in the blue-smoke haze from the burnt cigar hanging from his mouth. Took talent, coughing or choking or snoring but not waking, lips not losing hold on the cigar. Nearby on a chest was Nell's milk bottle, flaking white paint.

"Damn fool." Elephant Bill paraded about Jumbo's railcar, pulled chains, pretty sure from his hard words that he expected this to happen all along. "Getting between a wall and an elephant on a moving train."

Barnum was smiling placidly, but he always did, so it meant nothing, looking askance at Scotty on the cot, hard not to miss the soiled hay on the floor. Maybe it crossed his mind, he and his missus being such churchgoers, might not be ladylike for Nell to be cavorting with unmarried Scotty in a railcar, air stinking of man and whiskey, but Nell figured he was probably more relieved that the keeper of his star attraction wasn't inconveniently dying. Hadn't he been telling the American public for months just how dangerous Jumbo was? Folks bought tickets hoping to see it. Last thing he wanted was for that to be true.

"Little Eyes, we owe you a debt for saving our Mr. Scott." Barnum, sitting by the injured man, pulled a watch from his waistcoat and checked the time.

"Not me. Jumbo." Nell wrung out the linen in cool water and placed it back on Scotty's forehead. "Got right off him soon as he knew what he'd done. I just grabbed an arm and pulled. Some of the boys taking air on account of the train stopping, they hopped right in and got him to the cot."

Barnum and Jumbo stared at each other, only that pony wall separating them.

Nell wondered what the man was thinking. "It's okay if you want to say hello."

"What? Huh? No, no." He shoved the watch back into his pocket.

It occurred to Nell, for all the hullaballoo and bravado, the great Phineas Taylor Barnum was afraid of Jumbo.

"And what does Doctor Murphy say about our patient?"

Bill stopped his pacing at the foot of the cot. Scotty, motionless thanks to a hefty dose of laudanum. His chest was neatly bound—surprising, considering the doctor was a drunkard too—but seeping a pinkish-purple bruise.

"He knows about ribs," Bill muttered. "Seems to think some are broken."

"Good! Well then. Bill, you'll take Mr. Scott's place in the ring."

He rapped the floor with his bullhook. "Yes sir."

The showman stood. All was right as rain, he'd seen to that. "Little Eyes, shouldn't you be getting ready for the matinee?" As Barnum made his way to the railcar ramp, he glanced back at Jumbo, glowering in the shadow. "Bill, does he seem—our big friend here. Does he look...thin?"

"Most animals go off their food on the road, especially if they're new to it," said Elephant Bill. "He'll fatten up over winter."

JUMBO AND NELL'S MARCH FROM THE TENT AFTER THE EVENING show was slower than Nell wanted, Elephant Bill being deliberate about it. No one missed Scotty at the performance. How easily he could be replaced.

"Pretty song you sang out there tonight, Nell," Bill said all lovey-dovey, like he was sitting down to the Sunday supper she'd cooked in their house.

She tried to ignore him, walk up ahead faster. Rail yards never had any lights to them. Things happened in the dark that no one'd see.

"Not talking, eh? Well, don't worry. What we're going to do, don't need to talk."

Lanterns flickered on the side of the Palace railcar. Maybe the doctor was still there, hear her scream. And Scotty...what about Scotty? The accident showed her they were treading on very thin ice. If he didn't get well, there'd be no one standing between her and Bill...and Jumbo...short work that brute would make of him. And to think, once, she'd have been glad about that. Dora could laugh all she wanted, but Camel Girl had the right idea. Nell could leave, only she wouldn't come back, not as long as there was a bridge to jump from if things didn't work out. But where to go? How could she have a life that, in some way, wasn't just another kind of circus?

Elephant Bill horked a cheek full of tobacco juice and jabbed his bullhook into slow-moving Jumbo's backside, who grunted and snapped his head back with a scolding glare.

"You cut me tonight, Miss Nell. Makes me feel like you need to know how it's going to be. Don't you feel special? You know I could take any woman."

"Then why don't you?"

Bill grabbed her arm and made her face him. No foolin' in his tone now. "Because you're the only one who fights back."

The railcar door swung back. Nell pulled free.

"English?"

Standing there, face like ash, holding his bruised side.

Jumbo snorted, exhaled a great breath as Scotty hobbled down the ramp.

"Tell Mr. Barnum I'm well enough to take Jumbo tomorrow."

Elephant Bill jammed his hook into wood, grabbed Nell's arm. "You're with me. We got business."

He didn't expect Nell'd throw herself at him, fists out. Elephant Bill lost his footing and went into the mud that always formed outside of Jumbo's railcar, piss leaking out and all.

Too mad to even cuss.

She pulled the door shut with both hands, and knew that'd cost her.

ACT III

A TALL TALE

Pittsburgh, 1883

Rattling on rails…

Already mourned, the all-too-brief kaleidoscopic months of October to February, wintering and resting in Bridgeport. Acres of barns and sheds and huts, rife with chimney fires, the hammering of molten horseshoes, working of leather, shouting of animal trainers and cracking whips. Happy Jumbo, unchained, capering outdoors in a pen, his tusks a few inches longer, not quite mixing with his own kind but happy to be near them, fattening up in a daily game of toss the bread loaf. "First time we've ever had days doing nothing," Scotty beamed when he told Nell.

Then more rails…

After the launch of the 1883 season in New York. A stupendous month at the Hippodrome, burgeoning ticket sales, packed into a train, a hundred railcars pulled by four steam engines, one of which could be heard for miles—with the newly minted Jumbo Steam-Whistle—an itinerary of seventy to eighty shithole towns and cities, Scotty and Nell and Jumbo crammed into the forty-by-eight-foot–wide Palace railcar low enough to clear bridges, barely high enough for Jumbo to stand. And nightly, he wore his tusks down again.

Endless, endless rails…

Sometimes, only boys sitting on a fence watching the passing circus train. Or a wagon filled with a family waving from where tracks cut the road. The crowded balcony of the tiny town's only two-storey building: saloon, hotel, jail, and funeral parlour. Maybe a lone farmer on one knee in the middle of a cornfield, wiping the day from his brow, glimpsing the passing of something magical, and Scotty, weary, against the open door: "All he does is walk around the ring, and people, it's like they want a piece of him."

Or buy a piece. Black terracotta Jumbo in mid-walk, trunk raised. Mugs with Jumbo's face. A waltzing Jumbo extolling the virtues of Clark's Spool Cotton, trumpeting the cleaning power of Pears soap, hawking salt and sugar, malts and liquors. Jumbo carved from ivory, his name stamped on butter dishes, spoons, key fobs, sewing thread packages, cigarette cards, paper hats, neckties, playing cards, ladies' fans.

"Over a year now. Why do they still come?"

Through fields, hamlets, and towns shackled to plows, where souls suckled on machinery twelve hours a day, never having enough, never going to get enough, flapping moths hovering over kerosene lights glowing in hastily put-up tents, air so hot and heavy you could cut it. *Circus! Circus!* Freaks parading about inside with lives even the wretched could pity. And Jumbo, where twenty-five cents and newspapers' made-up fancies bought a few brief glimmers into an exotic continent. Jumbo, whose eyes must have once sparkled. Jumbo, who could only remember a time when iron did not bind. Jumbo, who could not see the blue sky of day or feel rain.

Scotty winced, as when the weather turned, and he hobbled on a leg troubled more and more by some ancient injury he took great pains to conceal. Burdened by a promise made of home, he asked Nell when she thought it would end.

She knew better than to answer.

AFTER THE MATINEE IN PITTSBURGH, EUROPEAN BROTHERS Marlo and Nico practised overhead flips in the nearly empty tent. Keeping to themselves, and too arrogant to speak English, talk was they were paid a celestial amount, which somehow excused the gossip that they were a little too cordial to be brothers. But the muscular men in light rose tights, which might have been red at one time, with belts of inlaid crystals, somewhat daringly profiling what was below the waist, hair in pomade and broad smiles of white teeth, got almost as many cheers as Jumbo and many more gasps from their flying somersaults.

Nell couldn't help but watch them as she and Scotty walked Jumbo around the ring. Scotty exercised the elephant when he could while Nell was having words with Jumbo about their performance. Sometimes he walked too slow, making her wave to the same face in the crowd, her song finished. Or too fast. Meant pulling up her skirts to keep pace. And she didn't care for that trunk of his to be sniffing all over, even if the delighted crowd doubled over and howled. Whether or not Jumbo understood her criticism, he was getting it anyhow, and always Nell delivered it with chunks of brown sugar and apples.

After a few turns around the tent, Nell noticed Marlo trailing Jumbo, holding the long pole used to set up the overhead ropes and ladders, silly grin on his face. A series of notches marked the pole towards the top. Nico was slowly swinging overhead watching Jumbo watch him and doing very little in the way of somersaulting. Marlo nervously nodded when he saw that both Nell and Scotty were looking, then scrambled up the rope ladder.

"Hungarians," explained Nell when Scotty questioned. "What do you expect?"

The incident was forgotten until that night when Armless Wonder fearlessly pushed his way through to Jumbo and Tom Thumb, lined up for the march of the elephants along with the trick riders and camel keepers and *children* climbing up the ladder to Jumbo's howdah. Armless Wonder claimed he was born without them, but everyone knew a Southern rifle shot them off at Antietam. He could do most things better with his feet, and that night right before the show was forcing everyone out of his way with his shoulders. Right alongside were the Burky Boys. Slow as tree sap, but good at pummelling the tar out of each other in front of an exhorting audience placing bets. Still, a bit of their storm-cloud faces got lost in terror, finding themselves unexpectedly next to Jumbo.

"There, Mr. Hutchinson." Armless Wonder, hopping on one foot, pointed the other at the Hungarian brothers with such anger, the toes quivered. "I saw them do it, right after the matinee. Mr. Scott was there. He'll tell you. They was trying to figure out how tall Jumbo is."

Scotty made that mistake once and only once. Kept getting asked by newspapermen sneaking into the animal corrals how big Jumbo really was. Got told plain and simple: no one measures that animal. No one photographs him. Orders from the boss. And if Scotty felt he wanted to tell those fucking newsboys something, he could say Jumbo's nose was as long as a python and he weighed as much as a freight train, anything but the truth. Truth didn't sell tickets.

Mr. Hutchinson, who'd trailed in Armless Wonder's wake, wanted to know from the brothers, was this true?

"No. We did not measure the elephant. Mr. Barnum tells us, no one measures the elephant."

Huh. Those Hungarians can speak English when they want to, thought Nell.

"Quite right," said Mr. Hutchinson. "Mr. Scott, did you see anything?"

Nell nudged him to keep his mouth shut. If Elephant Bill could get away with what he was doing, then so could the Hungarians. Circus people had to stick together, even with the shitty ones. But Scotty kept right on talking.

"Only this man here standing by Jumbo with a pole. The other one was above."

Nico and Marlo shook their heads and hands angrily. "We did not measure!"

"Newspapers offer a great deal of money to know how big Jumbo is."

"No, no, Mr. Hutchinson."

"They're lying." Armless Wonder was certain. "I got nothing wrong with my eyes."

Mr. Hutchinson patted the Hungarians on their shoulders. "My boys, I believe you. Too bad, though. Mr. Barnum might like to know that information himself. I expect he'd be grateful."

Jumbo heaved and swayed like he'd had enough of standing still, everyone talking about him as if he wasn't even there.

The young men broke into those broad grins of theirs that Nell didn't like to admire, and they admitted, yes, Mr. Scott had stumbled upon them trying to measure Jumbo. Now they'd do it properly, for Mr. Barnum.

"Ha!" snorted Armless Wonder. "I told you. Foreigners always lie. Didn't I say that?"

Mr. Barnum's partner wasn't the sort to get emotional about broken bones, old animals needing putting down. Just told someone to get a tarp and cover Iowa Jim when the kid got himself killed, and some clean sand to throw over the bloody stuff. Guess he got that way running the circus day-to-night. Ordered the Burky Boys to get the brothers back to their quarters, packed up, and off the grounds any way they had to.

Over hard-sounding Hungarian words Nell guessed weren't fit for the ears of children or ladies, Mr. Hutchinson instructed Scotty: "Give Jumbo an extra turn around the rings tonight. That ought to make up for these fools' hijinks."

AFTER THE SHOW, SCOTTY WAS ALL OPEN SHIRT AND SWEAT LEADing a reluctant Jumbo up the ramp. Jumbo fidgeted and twisted and poked his trunk at Scotty and didn't give a hoot about Nell holding out an apple. None of them liked going back into that dark, piss-stinking railcar. Then, doors slamming and whistling steam. Jumbo's trunk went right for the water barrel. Nell got out the milk bottle. Outside, yelling, wagon wheels, rope squealing on wooden winches, and animal wails and groans and grunts. Train would be leaving soon.

"Heard a telegraph got sent off to replace those Hungarians. Some place in Russia." Feet up on the cot, Nell poured a drink.

"Crowds'll miss those trapeze fellows. Jumbo too. Like they were flying up there."

Silence always followed a piece of Scotty's heart getting sliced out when the irons went around Jumbo's legs.

"Serves 'em right." Nell began her second cup, not bothering to remind Scotty he got them fired. "Knowing things takes away the magic."

ELINOR

Cincinnati, 1883

The coup, though partial, brought Nell no joy. Jumbo's name was still on the railcar, but the bed was again hers. Rather, Scotty's, but he was quite happy under a blanket wrapped in straw. She'd also curtained off a small table so she could bathe and set out her wigs and hats, and the rouge and powder that helped stave off the march of time. But no shaking the feeling that as soon as she closed her eyes, someone would come slithering in next to her, tongue out, reeking of sweat and tobacco. And while Scotty took more sense around Jumbo while the train moved, he and Elephant Bill battled like old bears over the elephant's care. Nell knew all too well who Barnum would side with if one had to go. All the while, Jumbo grew more restless and shorter tempered. Sometimes took another man or two to help Scotty settle him into the railcar for the night. He didn't sleep well either. Nell figured it must be the leg irons. Rattling and clanking all day, all night. Hide rubbed raw. When he did get down, splay his legs out behind him, not much room to stand back up. So early that morning, just Nell sitting against Jumbo's belly, watching the circus unfolding through the open door.

Cool breeze smelling of manured cornfields ripening in July was blowing through and although they couldn't see the flags on the corners of the railcar, they must have been fluttering up excitement. The town was big enough for a dusty mercantile, hotel with closed shutters, and a church praying by the rails. Just beyond, poles rose through the last bits of ground mist, criss-crossing the reddish-gold horizon. Jingling chains, snapping whips, elephants, snarling big cats, pacing horses, honking camels. Any animal that could push, pull, or carry was hauling and setting up wooden poles, rolls of canvas, crates, barrels, wires for the aerialists, tiered benches, wagons, and carriages. Wiry men with sun-browned torsos and dark rings under their eyes cobbled together corrals for everything else not caged or chained. Then the hammering of ground pegs, a gigantic canvas canopy and seating for twenty thousand swelling up like a dirty white mushroom, local boys running and jumping through tall grass, arms filled with buckets of paste and posters, making pennies by covering fences and lampposts and storefronts with tiny Nell Kellys beside oversized Jumbos.

She stuffed her pipe with tobacco. First time she did, Scotty gave her the look, enough to say London ladies, at least proper ones, didn't smoke pipes. She'd try to remember not to do it around him from then on. One of the clowns had given it to Nell, finding her after that first time Bill had his way crying behind the camel tent, mouth still locked with taffy. Said puffing on tobacco would make the pain down there go away. It didn't, and the clown went mad from the lead in his face paint, but she kept the hand-fashioned pipe just the same.

Scotty'd be stirring soon. Straw soaking with yellow-green piss had to be shovelled out. Jumbo needing scrubbing and feeding. Nell had long since given up trying to be ladylike when it came to gagging from Jumbo's shite. Scotty, working hard, dripping like he did, wasn't much for bathing. Got pretty ripe sharing that railcar with a man and an elephant. But Nell knew you could get used to just about anything.

Even the greatest elephant in the world who'd come to steal your thunder.

Imagine thinking on that icy April evening crowded down on Castle Garden Pier, she'd one day be having a smoke leaning against a Jumbo pillow, breath up, breath down, taking comfort in lungs probably bigger than her. Scotty hated when she did. Jumbo would never intentionally harm her, but as he and Nell both knew, one blast of steam or startling noise and the circus heavens would add another star. But that was Scotty, bristling over anyone getting between him and Jumbo. When his trunk came sniffing, Nell offered an apple from the folds of her skirt and quietly said it'd be their secret.

Breakfast for her and Scotty'd be a pour of whiskey. Clear up that ashen look on his face, though he did look mighty peaceful. That scowl under his moustache and the lines about his eyes smoothed out when he slept. Not a tall man, but who cared about that, and well put together, thought Nell. Surely it couldn't go to waste. It's not like animal trainers didn't have sweethearts. Lots of sweethearts. Just kept quiet from the women waiting back in Bridgeport with the children. Some fellows even had more than one. 'Course more than one was best left to Juggling Sam.

"Your Mr. Scott got a woman back in London?" Nell whispered, stroking Jumbo's belly. She didn't really want to know. Better to pretend the reply.

Jumbo wasn't much of a talker, but he gave good answers. If you listened. Nell blew a long plume of smoke, looking at that shirt of Scotty's come undone in the night, the dark hair on his chest, rough hands, lips hiding under his moustache. What would they feel like on the back of her neck, him doing things to her, being in her, just like Elephant Bill? Only thinking about Scotty doing it made Nell tingle and not want to jab a bullhook through someone's eye.

BECAUSE IT HAD RAINED FOR DAYS AND THREATENED MORE, A TENT was raised for those men from the *The Cincinnati Enquirer*. The reporters wanted to run a story on Jumbo when the famed elephant arrived in the city and Barnum, always eager to court the press, invited them down. The meeting was between the matinee and evening performances and the rain had started again, heavy drops bouncing angrily off canvas overhead.

Nell and Scotty were told to be in full regalia but not to say a word. Mr. Barnum would do the talking.

"We're postillions in livery," said Nell, fighting with an unwieldy umbrella on the way to the meeting.

Lately, she'd been reading to Jumbo from a book about rich people and people wanting to marry rich people. Both she and Scotty were surprised how her words soothed the elephant. She had a different voice for each character and was quite certain that Miss Elizabeth was going end up with the haughty Mr. Darcy even though she vowed to loathe him.

After Mr. Barnum regaled the reporters with fanciful tales about Jumbo this and Jumbo that, Nell and Scotty waited alongside the elephant for the rain to clear.

"Did you hear Mr. Barnum say Jumbo's gotten even bigger?"

Nell's damned umbrella wouldn't open. "I heard Bill say it's only because Jumbo's so thin, he looks taller."

"Maybe I should talk to Mr. Barnum about bringing Alice over—company like, for Jumbo."

The jiggling of the umbrella worked. It popped open. "Never heard you talk about an Alice."

"Not that he cared much for her in London, but I think missing his little wifey's got him off his food."

"How little could she be? She's an elephant."

"Compared to Jumbo. No matter, this time next year, Jumbo won't be famous anymore and we'll be on our way home. Maybe Bill's got some trick to get him eating for now."

Nell wasn't having that. "You know Jumbo, no one better. He'll eat when we get resting back in Bridgeport. Tigers are always skin and bones come winter. We all get fat by spring."

She was pretty sure Scotty didn't believe her, but she said it in such a way that he needn't bother asking Elephant Bill for anything. Still, hope of another winter reprieve put the first smile on his face she'd seen in days. Life on the rails wasn't like the Hippodrome show in New York. When those wizened and sunburnt scarecrows who made tents rise from foggy fields began pulling them down and folded the circus back into the steaming train, Jumbo followed in chains. Chained in the ring, chained in the Palace railcar, hobbling chains on hind legs. He'd not walked in normal strides since leaving New York City. Because Elephant Bill didn't trust Jumbo. Told Scotty he couldn't risk the elephant going rogue during a show. Had to always carry his bullhook. Killed Scotty inside a little bit every time, telling Jumbo, chains are for the best, then back to staring at a wooden wall with doors tightly closed because no one gets a free look, unable to fully lift his head, restlessly stabbing at the ceiling with his trunk, as if trying to find some way to feel the sun, see stars, smell something other than wet hay, excrement, onions, and urine. Night after night after night. If lucky, door cracked open to blurred fields of corn, towns and hamlets, flashes of light, and the possibility of rain tossed in by a passing storm.

Scotty wrestled with Jumbo's trunk and scrubbed his hide with a long brush, not gently, but tenderly, talking lowly, enough to hear sounds, but not words, like Nell wasn't there, but she'd make sure he'd know she was. Got out the drink, and so what if Dora told Nell setting her shoes under Scotty's bed would come to tears. Passing long hours reading aloud or playing cards until Scotty snored and Nell hoisted her skirts next to kneeling Jumbo and fed him apples. What was the harm in dreaming? Folks not paying to stare at her, Jumbo grazing under the widest bluest African sky, and Scotty being her man—

"Elinor," he groaned, one eye open. "Only person he took apples from like he does from you." He tossed his arm over his eyes like it was painful to see.

THE GALLOWS

Indianapolis, 1883

Sodden fields under weeping skies kept folks and carriages away and the main tent had so many holes, might as well be outside in the rain. Butterscotch in the air did nothing to cover the stench. Right at home up your nose, so you could have a whiff later and go off your food.

"He do something like that before?" Nell topped up their whiskey.

Scotty's shaking fingers cradled the teacup. Now and then, he glanced at Jumbo, softened by late-day shadows, quiet now, in their railcar.

Nell pulled off her wig. Wore her best to the execution. Golden curls pulled up behind, falling nicely on her shoulders. Like the sun shone through every strand. The hair came from a girl who'd died from scarlet fever and perfectly set off Nell's black bonnet and veil trimmed with pearls. Not real pearls, just painted glass. Now the golden hair stunk of burnt flesh and Nell felt sorry for the child whose hair she'd never wear again.

"You gotta stop worrying yourself, Mr. Scott. What choice did we have? Judge made us all go. Only end up in jail with Mr. Barnum otherwise, but nobody'd bring us meals three times a day from some fine hotel."

"Bill must have got tired sticking it to the gorilla. Took it out on Pilot."

One of the old Asian elephants. Swear to God, Elephant Bill enjoyed making that animal howl with his bullhook. Bleeding all down his backside after that show, crowds gone home. Guess Pilot'd had enough that night, turning on Elephant Bill like he did. Took most of the keepers to get him settled, but lots of the seating got busted and one of the young fellows new to the circus got stepped on. Took a few days, but he died.

Barnum was arrested. Judge said no death was going unpunished. Scotty worried. What would happen if the circus folded? He and Jumbo stranded in America, no way to pay passage home. Of course, he'd not be knowing how things work when rich people tangled up with the law. Nell told him that trial would be nothing but another show. Barnum granting interviews every day before parading into court like Jesus into Jerusalem without a donkey or palm leaves, his cell fitted out with velvet drapes and Persian carpets. Even had a bed and linens from the Grand Hotel. In the end, judge fined Mr. Barnum, but sentenced the offending Pilot for murder.

"First elephant I ever rode." Nell's voice crackled somewhere between a sniffle and a sob. "It's Bill should hang." And if Nell was on that jury, that'd be her verdict.

She must have said it in a rather peculiar way, because Scotty looked like he wanted to say something, then thought better of it.

The judge seemed to think circus folk were a pretty lawless lot and wouldn't be harmed by a little moral persuasion. Along with all of Barnum's elephants, they were ordered to watch. Guess the judge wanted the elephants to know that the good Lord gave man dominion over the beasts, not the other way around. So, Nell and Scotty and Jumbo, along with the other jugglers and acrobats and horse riders, clowns and boys who mucked out stalls, and all of Barnum's elephants, huddled in that Indianapolis rail yard, under wet streamers blowing dull and ominous from the west.

Pilot was already waiting, chains binding his back leg to the railroad track. Didn't take him long to sense the day wasn't going to end well for him, folks gathering in hats and feathers and coats all brushed and mended for a funeral, circus elephants being marched into a line. As that flatbed car fixed with a mounted crane was rolled onto the track alongside, Pilot wailed and pulled at his irons, began shitting himself.

Elephant Bill got his lads to swing a chain around Pilot's neck. Nell figured he'd have liked to do it himself, but Bill was hobbling like an old man with that bruised side he'd been favouring since getting caught in Pilot's rampage. With his wave to the man in the crane, Pilot, pulling so hard that crane almost fell over, was slowly dragged up.

Oh, that screeching!

If Scotty hadn't grabbed hold of Nell, she'd have fainted right into his arms. Even thought about pretending just that, not see the rest. All around her, shouting *stop! shame!* and shaking of fists. Maybe if those policemen hadn't been there, Pilot might have got saved, or a chance at least. But Elephant Bill ordered his boys to lay into Pilot with their whips, get him settled, and steady the crane. This time, as Pilot's feet lifted off the ground, the chains about his neck choked his bellowing howls into gurgles.

Jumbo stirred and snorted.

"Stop!" Elephant Bill was waving to the man up in the crane.

The chain holding Pilot to the tracks hadn't been loosened and as the elephant was pulled up, his distended leg was torn with a crunch from its socket. This time Nell dropped into Scotty's arms and as he picked her up, buried her face against his chest. The chain around Pilot's neck snapped and he crashed to the ground, dazed, struggling to sit upright, not making a sound as Bill ordered a double length wrapped about his neck.

Those watching turned their backs. Policemen hell-bent on enforcing the judgment, carrying out the sentence, but there were too many and when one got turned around, another turned back. Elephant Bill yelled at the keepers to have their whips and hooks ready.

"Oh, they must stop this." Nell buried her face against Scotty's coat and sobbed. "They must. It's inhuman."

"Don't you dare look, Miss Nell. I'll look for the both of us." Her wrapping of black crepe rustled under Scotty's hands.

Up went Pilot again, crying like a whole bunch of children, legs kicking. Swaying and choking, long minutes, swaying and choking, before closing his eyes; his tongue fell loose, and he swung.

"Whoa, Jumbo! Whoa!" Scotty roughly set Nell down, stepped in front of Jumbo, and threw up his arms. Jumbo took a step or two forward, shook angrily, lifted his head back and roared, the likes of which even Scotty had never heard. Folks nearby scattered and ran. Horses under the policemen bucked and circled, then bolted.

Jumbo slowly sank to his knees.

Even Bill sounded unnerved. "Jesus, look at them."

One by one, the other elephants followed. Trumpeting, roaring. Dozens of them, down on their knees.

Elephant Bill ordered his boys to get those bloody animals back on their feet, but for once, no one was having it. No more whipping today.

For a long while, Jumbo and the elephants made Nell and Scotty and everyone else look at what they'd done.

"ELEPHANT BILL LOOKED AFRAID, AND THAT MAN FEARS NOTHING."

No amount of washing was getting the stench of Pilot's carcass burning on railroad ties out of the folds of Nell's dress, but Scotty didn't care. Not about that. She thought about telling him to pull back on the whiskey, they still had a show to do, and Jumbo would need his full attention, but his hands needed steadying.

Scotty drained his cup, wiped his mouth, and reached for the bottle. "Didn't speak his name." Half memory, half growl.

Nell gave up with the stinking dress. Dora could have it. "What are you going on about?"

"Jumbo. Superintendent Bartlett, always making notes about him, put stuff in that science book he wrote, but never called him by his name. Just a *specimen*."

Drunk talk was coming, so Nell unlatched her travelling trunk and searched for the red corded silk. After what happened with Pilot, she needed something fun to wear.

"Bartlett told me his father used to take him when he was just a boy to the Exeter Exchange, near his father's shop. Old man kept a menagerie there, a lion, some monkeys. A bear. And an elephant named Chunee. A bull, ten, maybe fifteen years old, come to England from India for a stage play but got too big. Bartlett went whenever he could, liked to pet him through the bars. Took a cake out of his hand. Toss a penny in, Chunee would pick it up with his trunk and give it back."

Something in Scotty's manner stopped Nell rustling around with her frock and she looked back at Jumbo. Quiet now, serene even, but staring back at her. Made her shiver thinking about sitting next to him after what he could have done that afternoon. Made her turn away like she was partly to blame.

"One day, Chunee stopped eating. Just banged against a cage he couldn't even turn around in. Old rotten building, wouldn't take much to fall through to the streets below. Almost killed his keeper trying to settle him, so they had to put him down. Tried feeding him poison, but Chunee wouldn't eat. Word got around, army was coming in. Big crowd that day, everyone wanting to see. Bartlett came hopeful with a cake he was sure he could get Chunee to eat. Maybe even thought he could save him. Got pushed up front by all those people, had nowhere to go but watch them stabbing that elephant with bayonets, until a soldier put his rifle in Chunee's ear and fired."

Nell dropped the red silk.

"Mr. Scott...that's not going to happen to Jumbo."

"We pretend it won't, but that's how it always ends."

Outside, men were yelling, harness tinkling. Jumbo's ramp to the railcar was noisily put in place. Not long till showtime and Scotty could barely stand.

PET OF THE PETTICOATS

Lake Michigan, 1883

The still night air pressing down over the great lake followed the heat of day pressing down on men whose skin browned and blistered under cloudless open skies while unfurling the circus in Chicago. Lemon drops melted in their wrappings and could not be sold. Bears lay motionless in their cages. Like rugs. Nell rolled under the canvas wall of the tent clutching a folded blanket, then pulled grass out of her hair. No one noticed, thank goodness. She'd abandoned her corset escaping the sweltering railcar.

The back-and-forth beat of Jumbo's large ears fanned the inside of the humid tent, doing nothing but rile horseflies. He was chained to a stake. Scotty collected coins in a tin cup in exchange for the last few bits of his soul while folks filed along a rope and looked. The last of the day, a dirty-neck farmer and his three field-ripe boys, gazing up with a mixture of disappointed wonder, although with the youngest, possibly pity.

"Wish they'd hurry with some water." Only it looked like a bucket had been poured over Scotty.

His voice, these seemingly endless days of stiff muscles and worry, hollow. Best bit of happiness Scotty could find, so close now to the end of the circus season, was putting an X on that calendar hanging in the railcar, counting off the days until Bridgeport.

"Passed Dora on her way for a swim, says Bill and the boys are walking the elephants down to the lake." Nell unrolled her blanket. "You taking Jumbo?"

The back of Scotty's hand wiped his wet neck lined with dust. The tin cup jingled heavily. "Won't get him back on the train if I do."

Nell kicked off her shoes and pulled off her stockings then peeled down to her chemise and didn't give a what-are-you-looking-at if Scotty or Jumbo or the whole wide world saw. It was too damned hot. Just not for children pulling arms of fanning women, and mustachioed men buttoned up in waistcoats, red enough to burst. The ticket booth line for the matinee had been long and meandering while fresh dirt was raked over the rings, candles and lanterns lit, and a brother and sister from northern Italy spun with their teeth on ropes woven like a spider's web as part of their warm-up. Sold even more tickets after word got round that a tiger escaped and only the quick roping by one of the cowboys saved a German shepherd from getting eaten alive. James Hutchinson, who'd been standing near Scotty and Jumbo and Nell, shouted to the bandleader when that happened, You, man, play! A brassy loud Sousa—"Pet of the Petticoats"—struggling to be heard over shrieks and emptying bleachers.

A couple of lads carried in a barrel of water for Jumbo, spilling most. Nell rolled the blanket over herself. She hoped the boys would hurry. Drips soaked through. Jumbo was a noisy, wet drinker, or maybe he was trying to keep her cool pretending it was raining. Then night and silence fell full on, too much heat for animals to fuss. Too much heat to sleep. Too much to dream. Lie there and listen to night sounding like pages from a book being torn, then crumpled up.

"You smell smoke?" Nell shook off her blanket, got up.

No reply. Scotty, having taken off his coat, already snored on the other side of Jumbo. But Jumbo was awake, his legs chafing and pulling at iron.

"You can smell it, can't you?"

Nell stumbled over to the flap of the tent and yanked it back.

Jesus Almighty.

Orange cinders floated lazily about her face. The main tent across the way was in flames, fire spreading along burning ropes tying the circus together. The whole night sky was alight.

Scotty was by her side before she could call his name.

"Get him out of here!" Elephant Bill burst through the tent's other opening, distant bells now peeling from the city's brigades, men shouting, fire wagons sloshing tanks of water onto moisture-starved ground. "For Christ's sake, English, save Jumbo or we lose everything."

But Scotty's fumbling hands were useless against Jumbo's chains, stretched tight as he railed against the smell of fire. Elephant Bill cursed, ran from the tent, came back with an axe, and chopped, Jumbo pulling and bellowing, but the iron wouldn't break. Again. Screams, hollers, wild shouting as the main tent outside collapsed, sparks wafting upwards into the night, sending elephants returning from their lake swim panicking blindly towards them, trampling wagons and carriages and tents underfoot.

"Hell's coming!" Elephant Bill tossed the useless axe and ran as tent poles around them snapped free of their ropes and the now-flaming canvas overhead broke apart and floated on spirals of heat into the night.

The herd of terrified elephants bearing down on them, Nell held her breath, covered her eyes, and hoped it'd be too quick to feel much pain, felt the ground fly away below her feet. Jumbo had wrapped his trunk about her waist and dropped her under his belly, knocking the wind out of her. Scotty dived in alongside.

As the thundering wave of his brethren bore down, Jumbo held out his trunk, stiff as a branch, and roared, and roared, and roared, frightening the animals long enough for their trailing keepers to divert them towards the train.

"'...THE FIRE IS BELIEVED TO HAVE BEEN STARTED FROM A LAMP IN the main tent, which was completely lost in the conflagration. Mr. Barnum said the massive tent covered several acres and cost over $16,000, but the undaunted showman vowed those lucky enough to hold a ticket would not be disappointed. Thankfully, the hero of the day was the mighty Jumbo, who, in the face of the rampaging hoard of wild beasts, maddened by the inferno, secured his trunk about beloved Little Nell Kelly and pulled her from a horrible death.'"

Scotty carried on scrubbing Jumbo's rough hide with a long-handled brush, no interest in the Chicago newspapers' accounts of the near ruin of the Barnum, Bailey & Hutchinson Circus that said nothing about him. Or that he was even there.

"Mr. Barnum paid them not to mention you. We're in church country, and they'd have something to say about why I was in your tent wearing just my smalls." Nell carefully folded the newspaper in case he wanted to read it later when he thought she wasn't looking.

Scotty stabbed a bucket of water with the end of his brush. "Ah, it's not that."

"Then what?"

His sloppy washing wet his shirt, so it clung to his chest. "Stories like that make people think Jumbo's even more special than he is."

"He saved both of us!"

"And no one'll get tired of seeing him, reading shite like that."

ACT IV

SNOW ANGELS

Bridgeport, 1884

Locals would remember that April blizzard. Snow fell for three days. Mrs. Reed, who ran the Boarding House for Christian Ladies on Carlyle Street, and who told Nell, If you ask me—which sounded as if no one ever did—such spring weather in Connecticut was God's wrath because of waltzing. No good came of young men holding young ladies by the waist. Mrs. Reed sounded more wistful than outraged.

Nell scooped coal onto the fire. She'd tired of watching fences and streetlamps from the window disappear under white drifts when, by all ways and means, they should be done with winter. The room was warm if she kept ahead of the draughts. Mrs. Reed charged a dollar a week, a dollar and a quarter for a room with a private privy. Chairs against the wall kept the peeling wallpaper from rolling up, but nothing bit Nell in the bed, and because her room was at the back of the meandering patched-over mansion, she seldom heard rowdies from the nearby tavern. Best of all, no worrying about Elephant Bill. His missus and his kids kept him busy while the circus wintered in town. Here, she could do a season's worth of mending and warm her feet on the fender while she flipped through *Harper's Bazaar*.

"He's not going to look at you in either one." Dora contemplated the bolts of fabric in her hands, the red one looking orange when she held it against the gas lamp; it would be fetching trimmed with black fringe.

She often came by to help Nell with her mending. Dora's place was with the troupe across the street in the winter grounds: sheds and barns and warehouses where wooden animal cutouts march up pitched roofs, paddocks, jammed in, spread out, circled by muddy lanes when it thawed, tinder-dry creaking roofs under heavy snow, and a noisy roar of blacksmiths mending harness, practising jugglers and acrobats and clowns, old animals fattening up, new ones broken, spent ones carved up for meat.

"Lower the cut of that bosom another two inches, hide some ruffles inside to make it seem like you got more, still gonna do nothin'."

Dora meant, getting Scotty to do something, although he did smile more these days, and occasionally even laughed. This winter break had done wonders for Jumbo. For both of them. No longer confined to his railcar or moving from town to town, no hot tents and noxious crowds. Scotty kept him out in the big paddock, often with Tom Thumb. The two elephants had become inseparable. And Jumbo, devouring oats, bread, onions, and cabbages, grew positively and radiantly fat.

But Scotty still had no eye for Nell, not the way a man should look at a woman. Sometimes, he barely even noticed her visiting. In the evenings, by lamplight, he laboured on writing down everything he could about Jumbo. Got the idea because what Barnum was putting in the newspapers was stuff and nonsense, and some day, folks might like to know the truth. Not having much in the way of schooling, he said, he'd appreciate Miss Nell reading his smudged and childishly written pages. She wished she hadn't. If Barnum was offering fiction to the newspapers, Scotty had Jumbo lulled to sleep by angels. Informative was the best she could manage about the pages when asked, which pleased Scotty, and when he wasn't looking, she took the letter mistakenly left inside addressed to someone named Elinor, saying Scotty and Jumbo would be pleased to be reacquainted when they returned to London, and let it curl up in flames.

But no hiding the empty bottles. Scotty was still drinking, maybe even more, maybe because in Bridgeport whiskey was easier to get. Right under Barnum's nose. And giving it to Jumbo too. Medicine like, he explained, to help Jumbo sleep. Meant that if something really was ailing the elephant, lots of whiskey was covering it up. But for how much longer, Nell wondered.

Couldn't she see how fat Jumbo was getting, Scotty kept saying. He'll be strong enough to sail when Mr. Barnum books passage. Any day now. Long winter, who'd even remember how famous he was come spring? Just another circus elephant. The circus had lots. No need to keep him. They'd be going home, just like Scotty promised.

At best, drunk talk. At worst, foolish. Made up to get through days when worries are enough to kill ya, and maybe even an elephant. Kind of talk that, if he said it loud enough, and really believed it, might get him put someplace that didn't allow elephants. Maybe not even her. Saddened Nell to hear this dream, because one day the truth was coming, and no amount of whiskey was going turn Scotty's world rosy. So maybe he shouldn't be so sure about Mr. Barnum letting Jumbo go, Nell suggested as kindly as she could. She didn't have the heart to tell him Barnum's machinations were getting Jumbo bread sold in bakeries. A play about Jumbo in New York City. Roomy stagecoaches called the *Jumbo*. Jumbo dancing with a parasol on saltboxes, bathing on soap, and every week, a new song about Jumbo's life and loves and laments wafted through music halls. A name now synonymous with *bigger than big*. P. T. Barnum was making sure the elephant would be more popular than ever come the spring season. Scotty's dream be damned, the only place Jumbo was headed was back under a circus tent.

"Hey, where're you goin'?" asked Dora when it looked like dressmaking wasn't happening.

Nell was pulling on her fur coat. Scotty would have Jumbo and Tom Thumb out in the paddock by now. The coat was fox, trimmed with white wolf. A gift from Mr. Barnum. She knew he wasn't paying her what he'd paid her mother, and the coat was to keep her mouth shut about it. At first she wanted to cut it to pieces, but loved how it felt wrapped about her, and soon it'd be too warm to wear even if the draught and cold wind outside suggested otherwise.

"Don't blame me if they have to dig you out frozen and wait for summer to bury ya." Dora shrugged at the closing door, quickly taking Nell's place by the fender.

No point in letting a perfectly good fire go to waste.

NELL CAREFULLY STEPPED THROUGH THE RUTS TRAILING THE runners of a sleigh, then in the footprints of a man with large boots, until she stood beside Scotty, arms hanging over the paddock, barely nodding a greeting. Inside, Jumbo and Tom Thumb were tossing white powder over their backs and, now and then, making their way to the fence to snatch offerings of loaves and cakes from the townsfolk who gathered to watch elephants play in the snow.

"And to think I was worried about Jumbo freezing in these American winters," said Scotty, his pipe warming his face.

"Look, he's making a snow angel," said a girl with pink cheeks wrapped in her father's arms as Jumbo rolled back and forth on his back, circled by giddy Tom.

Nell unburied her face from the wolf trim. "Next year, Mr. Barnum'll be wanting to charge folks to watch."

Scotty angrily tapped his pipe against the fence, black ash whitening the snow as it fell. Nell wished she'd kept her mouth shut. He'd be thinking there was no next year.

From the road, two carriages, four horses, bells tingling.

"Company."

"Who's that coming?"

"Looks like...it's Mr. Barnum." He wasn't alone. Nell slipped back into the wolf.

"What's he doing here?"

Nell couldn't say, but it was unusual. Barnum didn't usually make the trip across town from Marina to visit his slumbering circus, not with drifts so high. Today he was wrapped in fur, tailored coats and vests layered like bunting, James Hutchinson tucked unhappily by his side.

"Ah, Mr. Scott, just the fellow! Come here, come here, young man. How is our very large friend today?"

Elephant Bill climbed down from the other sleigh as Scotty made his way over. Nell ignored him, but she was imagining his teeth grazing the back of her neck.

Mr. Hutchinson sniffled morosely from a miserable cold.

"I see a little snow hurts no one." Barnum chuckled. "Getting fit for the season, are we?"

"Jumbo is well, sir."

The two elephants in the paddock continued to caper about to spontaneous laughter and clapping.

"Good, good, what I like to hear. The thing is, Mr. Scott, we've a way to fill all our seats in the city this spring. Maybe even the entire season, when word gets out."

"But sir, Mr. Barnum—"

"The Brooklyn Bridge, my good fellow!"

"What?"

Mr. Hutchinson pulled out a well-used handkerchief and sounded like a honking goose.

"Am I speaking in tongues?" asked Barnum with a wide grin. "Surely even a fellow from the great England would know it?"

Nell did. No getting her anywhere near that monstrosity. Granite towering over watery shadows. Flimsy cables suspending roads and rails over the East River. A modern marvel, indeed. Made her queasy imagining those cables snapping. And not alone in her fear.

"The truth of the matter is, Mr. Scott, people are afraid of using it. They think this marvel of ingenuity, wonder of the ages, will collapse under the weight of horses and carriages."

"And it will." Nell was sure of it. Wasn't there a panic when the bridge opened last year, crushing people to death? But nobody was listening to her.

"What the city needs is something magnificent, something truly marvellous, to demonstrate to the people of New York City the marvels to come of this century."

Barnum paused. He liked to build anticipation. Maybe even use the word *marvel* again.

"I'm pleased to tell you, Mr. Scott, that the managers of the great Brooklyn Bridge have agreed to my proposal."

Mr. Hutchinson grimaced watching the elephants in the snow, as if someone had jabbed him in the buttocks with a hairpin. He blew his nose again.

"Next month, when the circus takes up residence across the East River, we shall not be ferrying the animals across on a barge. Oh, no. Our great Jumbo will lead the elephants across the Brooklyn Bridge."

Tom Thumb was tooting at a barking dog; those watching the stand-off laughed.

Nell couldn't imagine disbelief feeling any colder. Had they heard correctly?

"What better way to prove the bridge is safe than by having the largest animal in the world lead my circus across its deck. And you, Miss Nell, I've not forgotten you in all this! You, on top of Jumbo. Think of it! When has an elephant ever crossed a bridge?"

Nell imagined herself cartwheeling into icy water.

Scotty grabbed onto the side of Barnum's sleigh. "You cannot do this—please, sir!"

"Now see here, Mr. Scott—" Hutchinson's voice was thick with phlegm.

"No, no, James, let the man speak. Who knows better about Jumbo than our Mr. Scott?" The tight smile did not flinch on Barnum's face.

"It's...madness, sir. The people, there'll be so many."

"I hope so." Barnum chuckled again. He turned to the others. "Huh? Eh?"

"A loud noise? A ship's horn?" Scotty glanced back at the playful duo in the paddock. "What if Jumbo gets frightened and bolts?"

"Like I've been telling ya, sir," said Elephant Bill.

"Excellent points," added Mr. Hutchinson.

"There'd be nowhere for the animals to run. It would be too dangerous. Please, Mr. Barnum. Abandon this idea."

The old man nodded. "Manfully said, Scott, and I applaud you. But what can be done? The notices have already gone to the papers. Our Jumbo walking across the Brooklyn Bridge. Think of it! Not something the great city of New York will soon forget, eh, James? Gentlemen? And Mr. Scott, let's hope *my* Jumbo will have you by his side."

WALKING ACROSS WATER

Brooklyn Bridge, 1884

"Best leave those for me." Dora glanced over her shoulder at the silks and cottons Nell was laying on chair backs and spreading on tables. "Not like you're going to be wearing them after you drown. Look better on me anyhow."

Using a knife, Dora poked at the sizzling bread and cheese she was toasting in Nell's hearth. Mrs. Reed outlawed cooking in her rooms, and she'd know because there was nothing wrong with her nose, but the old lady was afraid of Dora and her sharp tongue.

The circus was readying to leave Bridgeport in two days for the New York City season and here was Nell, unable to pack a single drawer in her shipping trunk. It didn't help with Dora going on about a magician's assistant she knew who couldn't get out of a water tank during a trick that didn't go so well, and she heard drowning was like your insides exploded. Unless of course Nell got squashed by an elephant on her plunge into the East River. Probably not much left of her. Or if she landed on a boat passing underneath when the bridge fell apart, because it would, wasn't everyone saying so. Dora, who did seem to know everyone, knew a gambler in Hoboken giving fantastical odds. And Nell better wear her best, cleanest undergarments for when they fished her out of the river. They'd want to take photographs for the newspaper, unless her body drifted out to sea. Hence Nell's nightmares about floating dresses and sinking elephants.

"Tell him you're not going to do it." Seemed simple to half a cow.

"Say no to Mr. Barnum? He thinks me, being important, and Jumbo being so heavy will prove to everyone how safe the bridge is."

"Yeah, but he won't be there, will he?" Dora sat back on her knees and smelled the cheesy toast. Crisped to perfection. "Maybe you'll get lucky."

"What do you say?" Nell couldn't decide whether to keep the blue. It looked faded.

Dora handed a slice of toast to Nell. "Don't tell that crazy loon I took her plates. Or the silver. She probably counts them."

"Dora, what do you mean about the bridge?"

"Maybe it won't happen. Heard Mr. Bailey say so. Well, almost as much."

"When?"

"Yesterday. In the barn. Saw him and Mr. Barnum and Mr. Hutchinson coming out of Jumbo's den. Quite the head of steam on him too."

Nell took a bite of her toast but tasted nothing.

"Mr. Bailey's voice was very loud, said he was manager and no way was he allowing it. Too dangerous. If something happened, they'd lose not just Jumbo, but all the elephants, and how was he going to replace them with the season opening."

That toast wasn't going down without a swig of tea, or something. "What about me?"

"Oh, you too." Dora rubbed her hands over the flames.

But Nell wasn't as famous as Jumbo. Not anymore. And if she didn't go, there'd be a hundred Doras ready to take her place.

"Anyway, Mr. Barnum was giggling, you know like he does when he says he's listening to you but you know he's not." Dora raised her hands to shoulders and flapped like a baby robin, spoke with a nasally whine. "'Now see here, gentlemen, an obligation must be fulfilled! Already sent the bridge directors a draft for $5,000. The walk will happen!' Mr. Hutchinson, coughing like he does when he's taking one of his turns, he had to walk around in circles just to get words out. Didn't know anything about the money, none of them did. Said Mr. Barnum told them they'd been asked to do it, not paying for the privilege of destroying the circus."

"Or getting drowned." Nell brushed the toast crumbs off her lap. Maybe, hopefully, this would put an end to this insane foolishness.

"Mr. Barnum told them they were fretting like old women, the pair of them. But he called them boys. The looks on their faces? Made me laugh. Then he reminds them about buying Jumbo when they said he was pretty much crazy, because Jumbo was the best thing that's ever happened to this circus. Told those good gentlemen to put their faith in God. And him."

Nell put Mrs. Reed's china plate down. Couldn't possibly touch another bite. "Said all this, in front of you?"

Dora helped herself to the uneaten toast. "You know they got as much worry talking in front of us as they do a dog, Nell. But take heart. Talk everywhere, there's folks protesting. Guess some people think it's cruel walking elephants across the bridge."

But not the likes of me.

WHEN JUMBO'S PALACE RAILCAR ROLLED TO A JARRING STOP ON THE rails in New Jersey, the door didn't get swung back as expected, the ramp didn't get loaded. Jumbo's feet were heavily shackled, as were the chains about his neck to stop him flinging his head against the ceiling. Winter romps in Bridgeport might have dulled his hatred of the railcar, but he remembered quickly.

"I thought we'd have Jumbo marching to the river by now." Scotty mulled it over with the back of his hand rubbing his chin. "What's taking so long?"

Sliding open the railcar door enough for him and Nell to peer out, they watched circus men, carrying anything that might be used as a weapon, running and yelling along the tracks.

"Stay inside, if you please, Scotty, Miss Nell," instructed one of Mr. Bailey's men. "Trouble ahead, but we boys'll sort it."

"Trouble? What trouble?"

"That Bergh fellow's got his followers chained to the tracks."

"Who's Bergh?" Scotty watched after the men itching to mix with what was up ahead.

"Mr. Barnum hates him." Nell stepped back regretfully from the fresh air. "Though he's too much of a Christian to say. Made up a society to protect animals from cruelty. Thinks it's bad taking a whip to 'em and hasn't a good word to say about the circus walking elephants across a bridge. I heard he even has a wagon to pick up sick horses off the street, takes 'em to get better."

Jumbo, grunting, pulled towards the bit of open door. Scotty returned to shifting soiled hay into the corner, seemingly unbothered about their looming fate. Why wasn't he saying anything? If anyone could make Barnum hear anything near sense when it came to Jumbo, it was Scotty. The largest elephant in the world, and easily the most foul tempered, walking across a bridge, just as you please? So many people could be hurt. Or worse. Surely Scotty could argue a stronger case. But all he did was muck out the railcar.

Nell stomped her foot, then stomped it again, harder, when she got no reaction. "Don't you care what happens to Jumbo?"

"No one more than me, Miss Nell. You know that." The man didn't even look up.

"Then why aren't you stopping this?"

"Don't expect other men to quit making decisions for me and Jumbo because I say so."

Nell was stepping into her yellow taffeta behind her curtain in the corner. Not her best dress, but bright enough to spot her should she need fishing out from the river. Good thing Scotty couldn't see her anger fixing to catch flame.

"Very cold of you, Mr. Scott, having no care with Jumbo getting killed. Or me."

"If that's the Lord's plan, Miss Nell, I'll be right beside him until the end." Scotty made his way over to Jumbo, wrapped his arms in the elephant's trunk. "I know you're afraid, but they don't build bridges to fall down, and I've been thinking, get this behind us, maybe for the best."

Nell yanked the taffeta over each shoulder. “Only a fool could see that.”

“Folks sure to be tired of Jumbo after all this stuff and bother. What else can he do that people will want to see? And when that happens, Mr. Barnum will be sure to let us go.”

“Yes, like Moses, Mr. Scott, and that worked out well for everyone.”

WORRY HAD EFFACED NELL’S MEMORY OF LILACS IN MANHATTAN. Spring air heady with their perfume, and city effluent. Deep breaths. She tried to imagine fragrant clusters, anything to calm her as Elephant Bill’s men, armed and beating with truncheons, cleared the way for the circus animals and wagons through raucous Cortlandt Street crowds. More like a mob. Many came to cheer the return of the circus, and many more came to preach against the looming catastrophe. Ready to take up arms if need be. Human conceit at its most vainglorious.

Save the elephants! Save Jumbo! End animal cruelty!

Elephant Bill galloping like a general, shouting orders, snapping at any slow-moving animal or interfering man, woman, or child with the stinging bite of whip. Wagons and carts and carriages, snarling and crying bears and tigers and lions not part of the bridge walk, jostled over lower Manhattan cobbles wet with horse piss and dusted with apple blossoms on their way to the Fulton ferry.

The lucky ones.

Safe.

All while Jumbo, and little wailing and skittish Tom Thumb latched to his side, dodging the petting and rain of rotten vegetables, and the other elephants and camels, was swept onto Broadway, cheered and jeered by crowds with raised fists.

At Park Row, Elephant Bill broke his way through the rabble to Scotty and Jumbo, said there was trickery ahead and Nell would be safer up on his saddle behind him.

“I’ll ride on Jumbo’s howdah,” she replied hurriedly, even though torchlight in twilight, yelling and jostling crowds had the elephant pawing at the street, snorting and rocking the seat on his back.

"What trouble?" shouted Scotty from under Jumbo, inspecting the secureness of chains, praying they'd hold.

"Crazy bitch up ahead, named Cook."

Davinia Cook. Fancied herself a medium and, charlatan or true believer, afforded herself a brownstone on Eighth Avenue overlooking the park with her beyond-the-grave pronouncements. Well-known in her purple dress with black sash and heavy gold crucifix, she had convinced her followers of the bizarrely impossible: a dead preacher came back to her and proclaimed the Brooklyn Bridge nothing more than a figment of imagination, devil's work, and as soon as Jumbo stepped onto it, he and everyone else on it would fall to their death.

"Lunatics," cursed Bill, bobbing around on his horse. "No reasoning with people who won't see what's right in front of them. Worse than that Animal Cruelty lot. At least they know when to get out of the way or get trampled."

Davinia and her followers were lying cheek by jowl in the road ahead, currently in their umpteenth iteration of "Glory, Glory Hallelujah."

"Do we turn back?" asked Nell, hopefully.

Bill reined his horse around and tapped the brim of his hat. "Don't you worry, little Nell." His wink threatened to turn Nell's already upset stomach. "If these hysterics want so much to talk to the dead, me and the boys gonna make that happen."

Knowing Elephant Bill liked to crack skulls just for being looked at cross-eyed, Nell wasn't holding out for crazy Davinia and her disciples. Tom Thumb pulled hard on his rope, dragging Scotty, yelling, into the fray. She thought she saw Barnum laughing from inside a black carriage careening down the street, bouncing up onto the walkways, scattering old women and children in its wake. The elephant parade inched forward and the remnants of the medium's protest—limping, bruised, and bloodied, a ragtag lot regrouping around a torn purple banner—looked on piteously, hands clasped in prayer, as if watching the condemned march to damnation.

When the harsh electric lights on the bridge blinked and flared, illuminating the mild spring night, the boat-clogged river, New York City, Jumbo halted and trumpeted at the thunderous cheer, the chains hobbling his feet straining and rattling. Nell, clinging to her bouncing seat on Jumbo's howdah, peered up at the towers of the bridge, strung with iron cables, pierced with Gothic openings rising dark, and closer, the throngs on the street louder, rowdier. Lamplights and torches and blue-coated men on horseback with rows of polished brass pushed around them. Wild-eyed camels spit, their keepers clinging to harnesses, dragged on cobbles. Scotty sipped heavily from a flask he no longer tried to hide and swatted away Jumbo's wanting trunk.

"Yah! Yah!" cried Elephant Bill, herding dazed and terrified camels towards the bridge. The other circus elephants and their keepers pushed blindly forward, too many people to see where they were heading.

Nell thought about asking Scotty to pass up his flask, quick, before they reached the towers where some daring young fools hung precariously on the suspending cables. Elephant Bill was going hoarse keeping a path clear on the bridge deck through thousands, tens of thousands. More coming, swarming. Cheers and clapping reverberated over a river clogged below with boats and steamers, decks thronging with shouting, flag-waving onlookers passing back and forth under the illuminated span. A last-minute wave of protesting men and women surged ahead, locked arms, and tried to prevent the animals crossing, but the police on horseback were quick to repel.

The elephants and camels began their march over water.

Oh Lord...too late to start believing?

"Slow and steady, English!"

But Jumbo and Scotty, wide-eyed Tom Thumb visibly shivering, did not move. So many children, cheering for them, for her, Little Nell Kelly! Our Nell! Yes, *their* Nell. Sold by her mother to a circus charlatan who had the power to put her and all these animals in the way of certain death, and she couldn't say no, not that anyone would listen if she tried.

Nell wiped tears, hoped the facepaint held firm. How could they not know they were all going to die? Drowning! Nell hated the idea of drowning; she'd rather go slowly with consumption, coughing but beautiful. And in her bed. Glancing back fearfully at Scotty, it dawned on her, she'd never have the chance to say—

"If you please, English," snarled Elephant Bill, seeing as how the crowd was getting a mind of its own.

Jumbo gave a comforting *hoot hoot*, and Nell, ever the performer, leaned forward and patted the elephant's rough hide, broke into a wide grin, waved, and blew kisses as Scotty and Jumbo stepped onto the Brooklyn Bridge. A snort, a rolling head. Then another step. Slow and majestic, trailing the others. A slow-moving retinue across the East River. Seventeen camels and twenty-one elephants.

Underneath the upper deck, where the rail lines and carriageway passed, sightseers waved handkerchiefs, newspapers, and handbills, the bridge decking reverberating with untethered whoops and shrieks, hallelujahs and howls. Beyond the dizzying drop below that, the belching smokestacks from the steamers scuttling back and forth under the bridge, their decks filled with those glancing up, pointing up, circled by smaller boats, tooting and blaring horns.

And Jumbo reared.

Scotty glanced about his feet. "I can feel it! It moves…the bridge moves!"

Nell could, too, ever so lightly swaying: howdah to the left, stomach to the right. Jumbo growled at the unfamiliar gentle movement.

"Damn you and that animal, English!"

Nell looked back at Elephant Bill, battling to reign in his jittery horse but getting closer. Cheers became shouts. *Why aren't the elephants moving? Jumbo knows something is wrong!* The crowd surged to swallow Bill so Nell dropped low over the side of the howdah, couldn't believe her next words.

"We must go, Mr. Scott, or there will be panic! Walk ahead. Jumbo will follow you. Go!"

Scotty, not hearing Nell, ran the back of his hand across his neck…

"Hurry!" She waved to get his attention.

…and unsurely coaxed the elephant into a step.

Jumbo's on the bridge!

Another step.

Slow, lumbering gait, as if leisurely born to the view. At mid-span, the crowd rushed up behind the parading animals. Two cities linked and spread below Nell as Jumbo plodded slowly towards Brooklyn church spires and tenement flats, beaconed with lights. When a large passenger ship on the East River blared its long, low salute, Jumbo roared and bellowed in reply and Nell, quite forgetting herself, laughed out loud. *How marvellous is this*! Past worry, past fear, sitting up on an elephant's back, the greatest in the world, like no other person ever would again.

Jumbo's crossing the bridge and it holds!

It had not vanished, nor had the cables snapped, nor the span collapsed, but other than Elephant Bill, Matthew Scott was the only person on the bridge that night who suspected the hand of God in preventing a stampede.

Hurrah!

Nell saluted with a blown kiss. "You've done it, Mr. Scott!"

Who celebrated by draining his flask, his face quite pale. He pressed his forehead against Jumbo's grey hide as if hiding pain, taking no joy in thundering fireworks bursting and blooming overhead, drenching the river below with sparkling reds, falling whites, and dripping blues.

Nell, seeing Scotty almost in mourning, now regretted the price of their momentary triumph. Such a performance meant only one thing. He and Jumbo would not be going home anytime soon.

A SNAKING TORRENT OF TORCHES SURGED INTO BROOKLYN STREETS behind the elephant and camel parade, surrounding carriages and wagons in a raucous tide of laughing, shoving, and cheering, hanging from rooftops, out windows, porches, and clinging to lamplights as Jumbo and the other animals, whipped and prodded, lumbered and trumpeted and wailed down Fulton Street, leaving a wet wake of animal fear and trampled flowers. Jumbo swung his trunk left and right and bellowed. At his own name shouted, Scotty shyly waved. Nell tossed kisses, near death forgotten, renewed fame embraced. Folks square-danced on sidewalks and laughed and mauled jittery, frightened animals, poured beer down the throats of their angry keepers.

Elephant Bill, his horse stomping its way through the rapturous crowds, a deep V of sweat pooling down his front, reined up and grabbed Scotty by the collar. Leaning down, his yell was almost a threat: "Get these animals off the street as fast as you can."

Before the screams of the stricken mother, her child reaching for a better look, having fallen from an upper townhouse window, turned this parade into a riot.

GIVE FAME HER DUE

Ottumwa, 1884

"We'll sell more tickets!"

Mr. Hutchinson gleefully waved architectural renderings to squeeze a thousand more into the Hippodrome. And towns were added to the summer tour as the circus migrated west, filling more seats than pews in churches.

Meaning more long hot days under canvas, under garish flickering flames, choking oil fumes, and pawing, grasping adoration, loud bands, and Barnum's ever-expanding, audacious plans to show Jumbo abroad.

Texas.

California.

South America.

Always more, more, more.

"Clowns are lucky," Scotty once realized, before a performance. "Their smiles are painted on." He thought he was hiding well what was obvious to all—the cramped and fetid railcar was sapping life and obedience from Jumbo. After evening shows, Scotty had to use his whip and bullhook to force the elephant up the ramp and back inside. Nobody wanted to be around when that happened. Even Nell couldn't bear to watch the roaring, head-shaking battle of wills between elephant and keeper. A snarling leopard was shoved into a cage more easily. As the fits worsened, Elephant Bill ordered not only Jumbo's hind legs be fettered, but his forelegs as well. When inside his railcar, chains were also secured about Jumbo's neck to stop him knocking his worn tusks against the wooden slats.

"If it's the musth come back, we'll be ready," Bill vowed.

But Jumbo settled, Scotty drank. He'd beg forgiveness for what he'd done, look at his bullhook as if he wanted to drive it through his heart, and drink more. Like Nell wasn't even there. Heard nothing she said, as if It'll get better, you'll see, or The sun always comes up, would do a thimble full of good. Come morning, she'd pour a bucket of water over Scotty to rouse him, get him going, knowing that if he failed to have Jumbo ready for his performance, Elephant Bill gladly would.

WITH SUMMER TRAVELS, JUMBO'S WEIGHT LOSS COULD NOT BE reasoned away. Mr. Hutchinson and Elephant Bill often came round, faces stoic, heads shaking, not much being said. So far audiences didn't seem to care, not if Jumbo showed up for the price of admission.

"Some elephant ailment they all get." Every quickly dismissed rationale coming out of Scotty's mouth these days sounded mechanical, and full of hogwash. "Got him some fresh turnips. Loves 'em. Put the pounds back on, you'll see."

"Have you tried liver to get his blood up?"

"That's just being muttonheaded, Miss Nell." Spoken more from fear than anger. "Haven't you been feeding Jumbo apples long enough to know better?"

Jumbo may well be the star of the Greatest Show on Earth, but she knew what happened to animals that couldn't earn their keep. Cassie, the pure-white mare that danced with the clowns, went lame and got shot and sold for steak. When Major the lion became too arthritic to jump from one painted barrel to another, even being whipped so hard children in the front rows cried, he was left behind in a crate with instructions: *Call butcher for the enclosed. Invoice c/o Barnum, Bailey & Hutchinson.*

In Ottumwa, after a flurry of worrisome telegrams from Barnum, Mr. Hutchinson authorized Elephant Bill to fetch a veterinarian. He came back with a man who called himself Doctor Whyte, but to Scotty and Nell, climbing into the Palace railcar wearing a morning coat, he looked more like a preacher hastening to a revival meeting.

Even Elephant Bill sounded unconvinced, but "These Iowa farmers think highly of him."

Scotty asked if the doctor had any experience with elephants because the man was too afraid to get anywhere near Jumbo.

"Cows, elephants, not much different on the inside. They all fear God. Are you a God-fearing man, Mr. Scott?"

Doctor Whyte couldn't help staring at Nell. Then he hastily closed his floppy leather case and puffed out his cheeks when Scotty told him about the London Zoo and Lux-Bourquet and twisted molars. Could that be what ailed Jumbo?

The doctor saw no reason for his profession to be questioned, especially by a man with an English accent.

"Ridiculous. He's eaten something that disagreed with him. It'll pass. You'll see."

"Jumbo can't pass what he don't eat," Scotty admitted privately to Nell later.

Any further talk of Jumbo's health was derailed when one of the elephant cars went off the tracks round about Wabash and rolled down a hill. Could have been worse, but the railcar was empty. Jumbo and a couple of the other elephants were pressed into nudging it up the embankment and setting it back on the tracks.

"Commotion's got the animals all riled up, Jumbo knows. Smelling fear in the others, that's what put him off his food."

Scotty was grasping at straws by now.

Nell worried, watching Jumbo struggle up the ramp each night, but said nothing that wanted to be heard. Bumpy nights on the rails under the swinging lamp in the Palace railcar were fuelled with remorse and reeked of whiskey. When Scotty's whimpers dulled to a clutching snore, Nell spread a blanket over the straw next to Jumbo and stared up at the wooden slats that sealed them both in.

ACT V

THE WINTER OF DISCONTENT

Bridgeport, 1885

When the circus settled in for Jumbo's third Connecticut winter, Dora told Nell she was done playing the arse end of cow. She twirled in front of the mirror at Mrs. Reed's, holding up Nell's Dress of Diamonds. Really, it was only beaded with baubles, but it sparkled under the hot lights of the Hippodrome.

"You haven't got any talent. You'll always be an arse."

"All *you* do is sing—and if not for Jumbo, no one'd even listen. And maybe not for much longer. Jumbo gone, your Mr. Scott will be kissing you goodbye before he hops the first boat to England. If you even get that from him. You're making a fool of yourself, girl, running after him. Three years, and he ain't letting you catch up."

Sometimes Nell wished she could do without her friend, but Dora did have a way with a needle and thread.

"You're too fat to fit," said Nell about the Dress of Diamonds. She was screwing the lid on a tin and shoving it into her fox muff. Best way to keep the soup inside warm during the walk to the circus grounds. Mrs. Reed made the best soup—big chunks of beef, dumplings, the kind that clung to your insides during these harsh winters—but she only ever made enough for the guests in her boarding house.

"I don't understand," she'd say when spooning soup into bowls for the ladies about her table and coming up short. "I was sure I made enough for everyone."

"People forget things when they get old; it's perfectly natural," Nell told her, finishing her soup. She hated that Mrs. Reed made her sit on a pile of books and eat with everyone else around the table turning their noses up at her. Serves her right if Nell got her thinking she was going mad.

The soup was for Scotty. He and Jumbo were skin and bones—so much so, nobody talked about it anymore. Or afraid to. Just long faces and *yup, yup*. Elephant Bill and Mr. Hutchinson getting all kinds of telegrams from New York City. Those scared Nell the most. Jumbo did start eating when he was back in the main barn in Bridgeport, wintering with the other elephants, and even followed Tom Thumb into the paddock, but he just stood there. Soon, the townspeople who'd watched the elephants caper in the snow in previous winters stopped coming.

But every morning, Nell watched Scotty from the window at Mrs. Reed's on his way to a bakery near Washington Park. They made sweet rolls like the ones Jumbo was fed back in London. Made Elephant Bill laugh, getting wind of that. Walk to town to get a bun for an elephant? British were a queer lot. In this, Nell agreed. Most mornings, she'd see the bun lying uneaten in the snow.

By now, everyone's mind revolved around Jumbo whether they wanted it to or not. *How is he today? Will he walk? What did he eat? Have you tried alfalfa? Jumbo. Jumbo. Jumbo.* Nell wanted to scream. The what-ifs drove her near mad. Stuck in his shadow, even when she wasn't. How could she not resent him? Sometimes, she hated him. What if Jumbo died? What if Scotty left—without her? And from the looks of the man, if he stayed, she'd be a widow before she even got hitched, though she hated to admit Dora might be right about that ever happening. But as soon as she stepped into Jumbo's den—near emaciated, listless, dull-eyed Jumbo—all she wanted to do was throw her arms about his leg and feel his rough hide against her cheek and try not imagine the black hole they'd fall into when he was gone.

STOLEN SOUP AND BARRELS OF CABBAGES DOING LITTLE TO STOP man and beast becoming shadows, Nell suggested the howdah. Right there in the corner of the winter animal barn, collecting dust, *London Zoo* faint but readable.

"If, as you say, he enjoyed giving children rides, maybe he'd like to do it here. Take his mind off being in that railcar, eh, Jumbo?"

Scotty hesitated. "I fear the weight of that howdah. What if Jumbo stumbles carrying wee ones on his back?"

"Spring and summer tour coming, best you find out now if he can manage."

Jumbo giving rides to children? Mr. Hutchinson and Elephant Bill wouldn't hear of it. They'd watched Scotty battling to get him into the train at the end of last season. What if he stormed off during one of his tempers? Did anyone know if his musth had returned? No keeper could stop him then, and newspaper stories about kids trampled by elephant would be disastrous.

Barnum solved the impasse with a cable: *Offer Bridgeport rides on Jumbo charge fee.*

If something went wrong, they could only hope the New York press wouldn't hear about it.

"THIRTY CENTS!" SCOTTY CIRCLED AROUND HIMSELF IN WONDER when Mr. Hutchinson told him. "So much?"

"He is the most famous elephant in the world. A premium must be paid."

"When Jumbo and I gave rides in the zoo, I was allowed to keep the penny the children paid."

"Is that so, Mr. Scott? How lucky for you, now that you are in America, you're paid a handsome wage."

After folks read in the *Bridgeport Evening Farmer* that the great Jumbo would be giving rides around the elephant paddock, the demand always exceeded the seats on the howdah. Jumbo appeared to enjoy the exertion, only now accompanied by Tom Thumb's playful antics and not his wifey Alice like those days back at the zoo. He ate well, bulked up some, and Mrs. Reed's mental acuity was re-established.

The only one not grinning ear-to-ear was Scotty.

Seeing children ride on Jumbo's back now was a bittersweet reminder of halcyon London summers. Leafy walks, Jumbo nibbling coleus parterres, chased by gardeners. Kicking gravel provocatively into the dozing face of arch-enemy Obaysch the hippopotamus, dimpled from the harpoon attack that captured him. How the children loved that! Old Leduc, a fish in his mouth to feed his pet sea lion, Manon, who'd then kiss his keeper's bushy white beard. The pig-tailed macaque decorated by the Queen for service in the Ethiopian War. A Marabou stork that swallowed a cat. The tormented pelican who vengefully pecked out his keeper's eyes when he fell asleep. The odd-looking creature in the Eagles' Aviary from the Philippines that resembled an owl but ate monkeys. Folks in Paddington swearing the escaped capybara was a rat as big as a bulldog. On the slow way home to the Elephant House, an evening salute to Indian rhinoceroses Jim and Miss Bet, lolling in pools, while nearby parrots mimicked canal bargemen: *lick your spittle, eh darlin'* or *into the bushes, Mary!*

"Every time he sees that howdah," Scotty confided to Nell, that contraption in ropes being lowered, "Jumbo expects a turn around the zoo."

With snow piling in drifts outside the open door to the elephant barn and the surrounding Bridgeport rail yards, grey clouds threatening endlessly more, Nell doubted that.

THE VISITORS

New York City, 1885

When the circus season opened in the spring, Jumbo gave rides between performances. Being offered the chance to climb on the back of the elephant that had crossed the Brooklyn Bridge meant there'd always be disappointed children in an impossibly long line. Barnum even contemplated raising the ticket price to sixty cents.

"All this extra work and nothing for me. Or Jumbo. It's not fair," grumbled Scotty. Whiskey enough for an elephant didn't come cheap.

But no one heard this except Nell, before he was off to oversee the stowage of the howdah. Nell was in full regalia for the nightly Hippodrome promenade. It had become her practice to get ready a bit early so she could feed Jumbo, alone, usually carrots, before the two of them blinked blindly under the glare of hot lights and noise.

"You can't come back here," she said shyly, standing somewhat behind one of Jumbo's front legs when he snorted the arrival of visitors.

"Oh!" The woman was startled. "I was told I could find Matthew—Mr. Scott—here."

"He's off being busy."

English. The woman was English and concealed her face behind a kind of gauzy veil. Her brown hair was rolled and braided and tucked beneath a bonnet. The fussy sort of do adored by the rich with a maid. The front of her indigo-coloured dress fell in scallops trimmed with wiggling tassels. Velvet cuffed her wrists. Nell thought it a most beautiful dress she really wanted to hate.

The man with the English woman was much older, greying, and impatiently tapping his shiny shoe. A plain cream waistcoat stretched across his expansive middle, festooned with a gold chain. His chin protruded in imitation of his belly and his dark eyes were in danger of being swallowed whole by his fleshy cheeks.

"No further, my dear." The woman, drawn towards Jumbo, ignored the nervous man, her hand outstretched. "He is a wild animal."

"Not Jumbo. He knows me."

"Once, a long time ago, my dear—"

She lifted her veil. "Elephants have memory."

The tip of Jumbo's trunk sniffed the outstretched gloved hand, then up along the woman's arm to her hat.

"Really, my dear, I must insist—"

"He won't hurt me."

"Jumbo's never hurt nobody," said Nell rather indignantly.

"I myself once saw him avoid stepping on a child who'd tumbled in front of him." The woman smiled thinly, with great effort, like rich folks do, kind of indulgent and bored at the same time.

"Really, my dear, the smell here is quite intolerable." The man pulled a handkerchief from his inside pocket and hastily wiped his nervous face.

Jumbo stepped forward. *Clink.*

"Dear, old friend, those chains. What have they done to you? So sad and tired, and so very thin."

"It's an elephant, my dear. How can you say such a thing?"

Nell hung back with a mixture of awe and jealousy as the woman affectionately held the tip of the offered trunk. Whoever Miss-Fancy-Dress was, Jumbo knew her.

"Come, come. We must get to our seats or miss the show you insisted we see."

"Tell Matthew I was here," the woman whispered to the elephant. "And tell him...I've never forgotten you, dear, dear Jumbo."

The way she said it, well, took some effort for Nell to hate the woman after that.

Jumbo flapped his ears and snorted, the chains clanking about his back legs as she pulled a small turnip from her reticule.

"My dear—"

The woman nodded, stepped back, and pulled the veil over her sick-to-death-of-him face, but not before Nell noticed a tear.

"I would be grateful if you could you see that Mr. Scott gets this." The woman handed Nell her card. "We are not long in the city."

SCOTTY, HEADY WITH A COMBINATION OF WHISKEY AND ROSEWATER, pulled on the cuffs of his black coat and fumbled with his bow tie. Applause and cheering roared mutedly in the distance. The air was hot from the electric lights. He looked bothered. He'd been worried about Jumbo going out there, parading around the rings. Giving rides all afternoon, then noisy bands and screaming children in the front-row seats. Now, wondering about the small turnip he'd stepped on, like it meant something, confused by it being there. Nell thought it best to let her do the worrying for him, like she'd been doing night after night for months. Who better than she to know what was best to ease his mind? No need to bother him with a card from Lady High and Mighty and Lord Fancy Pants, giving him crazy ideas about things that were never going to happen. He sure didn't need to see the name, torn up and kicked under a barrel.

Elinor.

SEE NO EVIL

Baltimore, 1885

Rain bounded off the railcar roof and whistles of steam echoed hauntingly across the Maryland countryside. Inside, Scotty, steadying himself against the rocking of the train, lathered up Jumbo's hide, soapy water sloshing about their feet.

"...could send a telegram to New York City," he was babbling away quickly to Nell. "Ask them to put the howdah on the next train. It's the children. They're a tonic for him. Jumbo loves being around the wee ones, don't you, eh? Like back at the zoo, every day. I can tell he's eating more. He likes having children on his back. Always has. You wouldn't think it to look at him. Imagine, being afraid of Jumbo. Worked back east—and you remember how poorly he was. Between shows, get him off the train, fresh air, Jumbo will be—"

"Stop."

Nell stared into the bottom of her empty teacup. The sound of her own voice frightened her. The lantern swinging overhead deepened the lines around her eyes. Jumbo, leaning against the side of the moving railcar, raised his trunk and tapped weakly at the barrier to the rain.

"It's just that he hates being cooped up—"

No, it wasn't. "Take a good look at him, Mr. Scott."

What was the matter with her? Of course he looked at Jumbo, only what he saw was different.

When the circus train pulled to a stop outside of Baltimore, Nell angrily slid open the door, gathered her skirts, and climbed down. Or maybe it was that she was sad and not even Scotty got to see tears.

The rain had stopped, but the darkness dripped. Air, she needed air. To be away from his blindness. The inevitable. Elephant Bill knew it. James Hutchinson knew it. Barnum had to know it. Everyone knew Jumbo was dying. Only Scotty wouldn't see it. See Jumbo struggling, emaciated. Tied a rope about his neck so when Nell rode on his back, if he stumbled, she had something to hold on to. He'd just as soon lie down and go to peace if Scotty'd let him. And the worst of it? Scotty being the only reason Jumbo hung on, as if that animal knew how much heartbreak his leaving would bring his beloved keeper. Made more so painfully evident because she was never going to be loved like that.

"Nell?"

She wiped her eyes with the back of her sleeve. "Dora? That you? What are you doing out here?"

"Heard we might stop a spell. Thought you might like to take a stroll with me. Don't get to see you much, you being with Scotty."

"I'm not *with* him."

"You know what I mean." Dora slipped her arm through Nell's and pulled her along the tracks.

"You got some place in mind?"

"No, just taking the air."

Someone else, too, big and burly, stepping down off the train, crushing gravel under heavy boots.

"Who's that up there?"

"I don't see no one, Nell." But Dora held her fast as the shadow approached, feet stomping hard.

"Careful walking in the dark, ladies. Might trip and hurt yourself."

Before Nell could shake off Dora and run back to the Palace railcar, the man had his hand over her mouth, a big hand that covered her nose too. She tried biting, but he was wise to her tricks, fought for air as he dragged her between the cars. There, he let her breathe, but his thick arm was tight about her neck.

"You leave me be, Bill, or I'll—"

"What? Call for English? He can barely walk most days. I seen you holding him up."

"Let go of me!"

"Aw, c'mon, Nell. I've missed you."

No way. Not this time.

Struggling under him like she was, all Nell had to do was grab onto Elephant Bill's nuts and yank and yank and yank before he screamed and fell to his knees.

"You fucking little whore!"

Breathing hard, Nell pushed Dora out of her way. "How could you do this?"

"He made me, Nell! Don't say no to Bill. His missus is with child again and Bill, he gets backed up down there, you know that, but he's too big for me." They enjoyed, maybe a little too much, the moaning man, gripping his privates, writhing on the ground. "If I got him you, Bill said I wouldn't have to be half a cow anymore."

Nell picked up her skirts and ran. None of this was about Elephant Bill having her. He could have any woman. Took any woman. Had many women. It was because she said no, and the only way having her was going to stop was if he killed her. Or Nell killed him first.

"Nell, you get back here! English won't keep me away forever. Time's running out for that elephant. And you!"

Nell, not looking back, hoping she didn't trip over the ties in the dark, heard the man flopping around on the stones, getting to his feet, sounding like whatever was going to happen was all Nell's fault.

"You'll see! Mr. Barnum's making ready for the day, and a pretty penny he'll make when that damned beast is dead. He'll send English right back to London. Then it's just you and me, Nell."

She climbed up into Jumbo's railcar and pulled the door shut behind her, leaned hard against it, closed her eyes, and wished she could quickly undo her stays, like she hadn't had a breath in all that time. Scotty sleeping, or drunk in the straw, didn't even stir. Jumbo, large eyes sad and rheumy, stared at the floor, like he contemplated going down but feared not getting back up.

DURING AN AFTERNOON PERFORMANCE IN CINCINNATI, JUMBO WAS so frail Scotty couldn't coax him into the ring.

"Use your bloody hook, man, or I will," threatened Bill, pacing about, ready to take over.

Scotty jabbed hard, but the groan was his, as if he'd impaled himself with the hook. No roars from Jumbo, no head-tossing anger, just a long, sad look ahead at grinning, gawking faces lining bleachers before taking a slow, plodding step, then another, then another. Somersaults spun on ropes overhead, tigers snarled, clowns honked tin horns, and stallions pranced. Nell waved and blew kisses, promising herself, next performance, she was getting one of the clowns to paint her a smile. Then Scotty doubled over and emptied his stomach, or would have, had he eaten anything.

"You sing now, Miss Nell…real good," Scotty said hoarsely, wiping his mouth. "Then nobody'll notice he can't make it around the ring."

AFTER THE PERFORMANCE, MEN GATHERED UNDER STARS OUTSIDE the main tent. Nell, keeping out of Elephant Bill's sight, stroked Jumbo's trunk, offered an apple. Green one. He liked those best. At first accepted, then dropped. Inside the tent, swinging and flying aerialists made the crowd applaud wildly. Nell knew the situation was grave when the money man came to see for himself.

"Do we know what's causing his illness?" asked Mr. Hutchinson.

Scotty said someone had tried to poison Jumbo once before, in London. Maybe that was it.

"Take a helluva lot of poison." Bill was head elephant man. He wasn't listening to anything Scotty had to say. "No, something else is wrong."

Jumbo, waiting for Scotty and Nell to return him to the railcar, stared impassively at the men staring at him. Mr. Hutchinson shuddered, unnerved, turned his back. “Hate to be the one to say this, but we’d better prepare for the worst.”

Scotty flung his bullhook to the ground, like being party to its use scalded his soul, blocked the elephant defiantly from despair. If anyone thought he’d accept this sentencing, they were fools. “Let Jumbo die?”

Bill sniggered—over the death of an animal.

“Now, now, Mr. Scott. Let’s not start chiselling granite just yet. But Mr. Barnum needs to be told. I’ll cable him in the morning.”

“What about Jumbo?”

“We’re a few days out of Detroit. I’ll see that we get a veterinarian to have a look.”

Scotty nodded stiffly, holding back that he just might break. “A proper doctor, Mr. Hutchinson. One who knows the difference between an elephant and a cow.”

WHAT A LEGEND NEEDS MOST

St. Thomas, 1885

Scotty pulled himself from out of the hay. Jumbo, nubs of ivory chafing against wood siding, laboured upright in wheezing frustration. The railcar pitched with his efforts. Painful, Nell turned away.

Through the grimy window, slanting early light. Mid-September light. Men in thick plaid who only hours before had folded up the circus after the show in Chatham, Ontario, unloaded the train while morning mist snaked through grass. By midday, mist and shirts would be gone.

"Where are we?" Scotty sounded hoarse, groggy, almost bewildered at having to repeat another day.

Nell pulled her shawl against the morning cool. "St. Thomas."

East of Detroit, in Canada, near the shore of Lake Erie. Two performances, matinee and evening show. But Nell dreaded playing here. The rail junction was in the centre of town. No room for a hundred circus cars and all its animals, dozens of elephants to unload. Everyone would have to travel to the next junction to cross over the tracks then walk back to the tents already rising near Miller Street. A long walk back in the dark after the evening performance, where a man with a score to settle could wait unseen.

To many, Jumbo looked to tower ever taller. "The circus agrees with him," Barnum trumpeted. "He grows even larger!" It was an illusion caused by Jumbo's skeletal frame. The veterinarian in Detroit, barely out of short pants, eager and star-struck—*jumpin' Jehoshaphat, he is a big 'un*—found nothing, or, as Nell suspected, knew nothing.

She had to plead with Scotty that no matter what others wanted to believe, or whatever the doctor said that Scotty needed to hear, Jumbo was too weak to make that long walk from the train to the fairgrounds twice in one day. Barnum, Elephant Bill, doctors—of them all, Scotty was hardest of hearing. Audiences might cheer, but every night, Nell and other circus people sadly gambled on Jumbo making it around the ring. And what the Greatest Show on Earth without Jumbo would mean to her was never far from Nell's thoughts.

Now, having stood, he swayed.

If he gets through the day...again tomorrow...one day closer to Bridgeport and winter rest. If he makes it. Please let him make it. Just one more. Hours spent worrying—and over an animal, something Nell had vowed never to do again. Piece of you always got ripped out when they died, even if you tried hard not to love.

DURING THE MATINEE IN ST. THOMAS, A HORSE RIDER TUMBLED AND got run over in a chariot race. Children cried and parents covered their eyes. A woman fainted and two men carried her from the tent. The rider's mangled body lay on a crate covered by a blanket waiting for the town's undertaker who was in the stands and wanted to see the end of show. But no superstition was preventing the evening performance, especially when news travelled of the bloody carnage, selling out the last few tickets.

Scotty asked if Nell knew the deceased.

No. But the accident reminded her of Iowa Jim.

Bad omens put everyone on edge getting ready for the evening show, and a death during a performance made even the animals jumpy. Maybe that's what put Elephant Bill off jabbing King Mykonos with a stick through the bars of the gorilla's cage. Instead, he was talking to that stranger, hands moving and waving. Not like Elephant Bill at all. At first Nell thought he was angry, but the more she watched him, it was as if Bill was explaining something. Lots of detail. The man: thick arms and shoulders, hat, suitcase, like he'd just come off a train. And when Bill caught sight of Nell paying attention, he glared back, took the man by the elbow, and led him away.

For the evening performance, Nell chose her blood-orange silk. The dress was too pretty and too fine to wear often. Added the red-hair wig laced with pretend pearls. Satin gloves to her elbows and those gorgeous new yellow pumps Montmorency had gone through great pains to craft for her. All she had to do was get through the show without stepping in Jumbo's shit—that is, if Jumbo could get through the show at all.

Nell entered the ring by his side, singing "All the Way My Savior Leads Me" but mostly getting drowned out by the band, Tom Thumb begging sweets tossed from an appreciative audience blissfully believing everything was hunky-dory. Jumbo even kept up and Scotty didn't have to use his bullhook. Tonight, Jumbo was unusually sweet, playfully jabbing Nell with his trunk, securing her arm like they were promenading, even circled her waist and she tapped him loose with her fan. Country folk loved the antics. Only once did she notice Elephant Bill at ringside standing with his mute and uninterested guest, but he looked distracted. Behind Jumbo followed Toung Taloung, billed as the white Burmese elephant, who really wasn't white at all. More like splotchy light grey, which is probably why everyone still cried:

Jumbo!

Jumbo!

Jumbo!

The audience had barely left their seats when circus men began knocking down the tents and folding up the caravans. Nell wished she'd remembered to bring her shawl. Days got hot, but this far north September nights quickly took an autumn chill. The elephants and other animals were already making the long walk back to the circus train.

"Evening, Miss Nell. Looking fine." Elephant Bill tapped his bullhook to his hand.

She could feel the grind of her back teeth, how he flummoxed her, wondering if ever there'd be a day when that wasn't so. Nell tucked her arm behind Jumbo's leg, had no intention of letting go until the door to the Palace railcar slammed shut.

"Good show tonight, English."

The compliment from that man was a first, made Scotty grin like a fool. Elephant Bill could be nice like that, fill your mouth with saltwater taffy.

"Had me a word with the yardmaster," he said. "He's going to let us take down some of that fencing. You get Jumbo and Tom over the tracks, shorter walk back. No trains coming tonight. Just make sure he's got his chains on."

Nell warned Scotty about listening. Not like Bill to be sweet like cherry pie. "Or caring about an animal," she mused after he'd left them to see to the fence, Scotty lighting some lanterns.

"You sure you want to come with us? Dark on those rails, and you not being dressed for it."

Then again, she wasn't walking alone, and hurriedly followed Scotty and the elephants through the hole made through pulled-down boards.

"Good of Bill. We can take our time. Slow walk'll do him good." Scotty guided Jumbo and Tom Thumb onto the tracks.

"Night gets thick out here." Nell rubbed her arms. "And cold."

A long row of railcars sat idle on the siding next to them. On the other side of the track, a hill rolling down in the dark but no seeing how far. Nell waved her lantern. Looked deep, guessing by not seeing where it ended. Faint light came from the circus train up ahead and the whipping, grunts, and groans of animals being loaded sounded closer than they were. Hopefully, walking across the ties wouldn't ruin her yellow shoes, but just in case, Nell slipped them off and held them in her hand. Tom Thumb, thinking food, tried to snatch them.

"You know, Miss Nell, Bill was right; it was a good show tonight. Did you see Jumbo playing with wee Tom near the end? Like that first time, back in New York."

Stepping from one tie to the other wasn't easy, not while holding the lantern and the edge of her dress. "Wasn't I right beside them? Even with this light it's hard to see out here."

"Stay on the tracks, Miss Nell, and we'll be fine."

Jumbo lumbered slowly behind, the *swish swish swish* of his great Africa-shaped ears, long, deep, soothing breaths, a snort, afraid-of-the-night Tom Thumb scrambling in tow.

Muted voices flowed back from men ahead, laughing, doors shunting open, creaking shut. The tinkling of harnesses. Kind of calming after the brightness and din under canvas.

"He's getting better, Miss Nell. I know it. I didn't need to hook him even once."

What Nell heard was Scotty convincing himself. Trying to.

"And you know, I heard Mr. Hutchinson say Mr. Barnum wants to take the circus to London."

"Mind what you pay attention to. Mr. Barnum says lots of things." Nell, sure she heard something, pointed the light into the black behind them, seeing only Tom Thumb, wide-eyed and skittish out there alone as she. Were there bears, Nell wondered.

"But once we're back in England, not much farther to Africa. And you know, I've been giving some thinking to this. You know how Mr. Barnum likes to read about himself in the papers? Lot of goodwill, I expect, for him getting Jumbo home."

"Goodwill, yes—money, no." Nell, juggling skirt and shoes and a lantern, and imagining things in the night she didn't want to, hissed in frustration at their lack of progress. "You believe Bill about the trains?"

"You heard him. Elephant Bill can't be all bad—"

"Look at Jumbo now! What's he doing? Best hurry him, Mr. Scott. No time for lollygagging at the stars."

Scotty flashed his lantern into Jumbo's face. "Why that he is, Miss Nell."

Brilliant as they were, and clear and endlessly spanning the night over them. Used to be, Nell was a star, not tearing her stockings on rough bits of wood. "Oh, do hurry. Boys'll be waiting up ahead to get us loaded."

But Jumbo had unexpectedly wrapped his trunk about his keeper's waist, held him firm, pulled in the man's face intimately. Delighted, Scotty giggled like the boy he might have once been. Nell wanted to look away but couldn't, sad and a bit hurt because this moment wasn't meant for her. They never were. She brushed off envious tears and the foolishness of worry causing them.

But there, again, something grumbling, like distant thunder. But there were so many stars.

Nell shone her lantern at the track behind them, held it high. "You hear that?"

Scotty disentangled himself from Jumbo's grasp. "Dog from town? You saw them sniffing around the tent."

"Listen."

"Miss Nell, you're getting yourself all worked—"

"Be still, Mr. Scott!"

Nell put her hand on the iron rail. It faintly vibrated. She tied up the ends of her blood-orange skirts around her waist and skipped back along the railway ties until she was behind Tom Thumb who thought she'd come to play.

A light: faint, distant, growing brighter.

"It's a train!"

"Can't be. Bill told me to bring Jumbo—"

"Get him off the track!"

A sharp whistle wailed through the night—louder, blaring, wheels rattling on the tracks. Nell's cry alerted men loading the circus train up ahead.

Lights beamed down towards them and shouting: *Jumbo's down there on the tracks!*

"Mr. Scott!" Nell started running.

But Jumbo stood firm.

"He won't go down into the ditch!"

"Make him—hurry!"

Lights from the fast-moving train shone on them, its horn wailing in warning and sharp brakes screeching with a metallic pitch as wheels skidded along iron. Jumbo was bathed in an aura from the freight train's light.

It can't stop.

"Move, damn you, Jumbo! Move!"

But large, watery eyes chose to gaze at the stars, as Scotty thrust the bullhook that he had spared all evening like a harpoon into Jumbo's hide, again and again, until the elephant calmly wrapped his trunk around his keeper's thrusting arm and held firm. He glanced back at the coming light, then at Scotty, who turned to Nell and mouthed the words, *Save yourself.*

ACT VI

SKIN AND BONES

RMS *Etruria*, 1889

The October ocean sprayed across the tossing bow, dousing the man slipping across the rolling deck to the railing where, grabbing tight, whatever the poor soul had in his stomach went over the side. Reminded Nell of Barnum's boy with all the Ls. Funny, she hadn't thought about Lew in years. She pulled the blanket tight about her. Messy way to die.

The man at the railing wiped his mouth with the back of his hand, braved the swells over to Nell who had her pick of deckchairs in the glassed promenade. Second-class ladies feared broken feathers or losing hats to the wind.

"Another drink, madam?" He rubbed sea from his face.

Nell liked this steward. Maybe Italian or Armenian, possibly even Greek; the sort of sullenly handsome twentysomething with bluish cheeks who'd be fat and bearded by forty. Didn't look at her like she was something to be stared at, or maybe with his duties, he'd seen it all. Train travel being ruined for Nell after Jumbo's accident, and now travel by steamer after what happened at the dock, the man didn't bat an eyelid when she said a whiskey would do the trick to calm herself after watching those wretched zebras.

Happened while Elephant Bill and his crew roughly herded scared and skittish circus animals along the dock to the gangplank. The dockside was busier than usual; folks come to watch: not every day an entire circus got loaded into a ship. Animals in crates and cages waiting their turn. Wagons piled with trunks and travel cases. Never one to care about delicate sensibilities, other women passengers covered their ears from what came out of barking Bill's mouth, but just the sight of him on shore, and soon to be onboard, reduced Nell to angry tears. And with Scotty mostly too drunk these days to even button his coat, let alone protect her, she could soil herself like an infant at the thought of days on the ocean with nowhere to hide, Bill with time on his hands. When the loud blast from a nearby tug startled the zebras on the narrow gangplank, three of them jumped the railing and plunged into the icy black water.

Mr. Barnum, who'd been on deck with his wife, Nancy, watching as his animals were loaded, shouted in a voice Nell seldom heard, See here, Bill, those beasts came all the way from Zululand at great expense, I can't have them lost.

The horse-like animals with wide white stripes charmed circus audiences while running around the rings, a Pekingese jumping from one back to another. Dogs being easier to come by than wild zebras, there was always one being trained in case of a runaway or fatality.

Stevedores scurried under Bill's foul temper, tossing barrels and swinging rope, frantic to find a boat suitable to fishing jumpers out of the harbour. Bloody bastards thinking they're going to swim back to Africa, Bill snarled, one of those rare moments he looked to be bothered. When a boat finally launched, two of the zebras already floated lifelessly. The last one, making that ungodly cry, fighting any attempt at getting roped. Only time Nancy Fish Barnum said a kind word to Nell was when Elephant Bill, frustrated, emptied his pistol into the animal, leaving Nell shaken, imagining herself floating in the water. Was Nell going to be all right? Mrs. Barnum sounded surprised, like maybe it was out of sorts to be upset over these animals dying. Or maybe it was just that Mrs. Barnum was worried about her husband losing another moneymaker on the same day. By then the captain of the *Etruria*, alluding to a schedule, was pulling away from the wharf.

No doubt the animals would be stuffed and mounted. *Exotic zebras! Yours to mourn for the price of admission.* Nell had witnessed it once before, in the dining room at the Park Avenue Murray. Head table groaning under hothouse roses. Chandeliers and crystal globes and turkey necks cinched with diamonds. But not zebras—Jumbo. Phoenix rising from choking smoke and burning flesh…

…through hissing, hot steam, blinking lanterns. Crying, wailing, a child. No, Tom Thumb. Down here, he's down here! He's alive! Christ, look at his leg…get a rifle. Here! Over here! Look! I got me a souvenir, a piece of his ear! That man with the suitcase who'd been talking to Elephant Bill, what's he doing? Why is his apron stained with blood? Jesus, he's still alive! Jumbo's still alive! Scotty bargaining with gods and devils. Don't look. Men turn from men who cry. Who've you got there? Some kid. I saw it, he saved them, Jumbo tossed her and Scotty out of the way. He saved their lives! You, run, find a doctor! Go! Oh, Christ, that's Miss Nell…me, it was me…Carried like a doll in a man's arms…

…Bring Governor Hill a brandy, Barnum was saying, like the luncheon was a party and not a wake. Do you kneel, or bow, or genuflect before such a stately luminary? What about the new idols of the age? Jumbo's massive skeleton to the left towering to a few inches of the ceiling; 1,500 pounds of skin covering metal and wood to the right. Staring glass orbs that didn't see, but saw. The two Jumbos. Honours to the man Ward, professor and taxidermist, cutting before the fires were out and heart still beat.

So soon, asked the governor? How was that managed?

Yes, Mr. Barnum, how was *that managed?*

The boys of the press never ask the right questions, but why answer when there are gifts—ivory medallions sliced from tusk, mounted in round blue satin boxes, gold and engraved—and luncheon, served with Jumbo's ivory powdered in the jelly. A delicacy devoured by Park Avenue aristocracy.

Blessing in disguise, speechified Barnum. Who needs the cost and worry of an ailing, recalcitrant eleven-foot giant when you can wheel out two for the price of one? Skin and bones. A deal at one thousand dollars. Look! See where the train ripped off the hide? Nice stitching. And Alice, beloved Alice, dubbed Jumbo's dear wifey, bought from the London Zoo for peanuts to round out the bill; no crowd for her when she hovered and squealed over the New York City dock. Scotty's mournful reunion in the Hippodrome. Top hat, new coat. Lord Matthew Scott. Morose and tottering. Alice, trumpeting, pulling against her ropes, knowing that monstrosity on wheels was no mate of hers. Yes, poor, silly Alice. Nell watched her from the Boarding House for Christian Ladies when the elephant barn in Bridgeport caught fire in '87, running in circles, trying to put herself out in the snow.

The present buffeted the *Etruria* with a roll.

No one watching, Nell pulled out another cigarette. Where was that man with her whiskey? First class probably got the stewards with sea legs.

And champagne. Lots of champagne. Barnum and that Nancy, they'd be sure to have champagne with dinner. Might even have grudgingly offered Nell a glass, but no way was she accepting the invitation to dine. Being stared at in the middle of three rings was one thing; during three courses without recompense was quite another. Nancy Barnum couldn't understand why Nell made such a fuss about sailing with them and Jumbo's hide and skeleton to London, and not getting off to travel with Elephant Bill and the rest of the circus now that the delay forced them to go on a cargo ship. But she did cast her nose over her shoulder at Nell and insisted, Do join us for dinner, if you must. The snotty woman could choke on a fishbone for all Nell cared.

No, she'd weather it out here on the promenade, choking under ash plumes from the ship's stacks, head aching from the *poom-poom-poom* pulse of the engine. Plans had to be made, and plans don't make themselves. Watching Bill pull those carcasses out of the harbour convinced Nell—mounted under glass, holding a dove, perpetually smiling? Skin and bones? No. When the circus returned to New York from London in the spring, it'd be without her. Barnum just didn't know it yet. The steward finally appeared with Nell's whiskey, and she held out her cigarette for him to light.

MAYBE, ONCE UPON A TIME

RMS *Etruria*, 1889

Scotty was mesmerized by grey waves rolling and tossing into foamy caps of white under low, sunless, bird-less skies. So much... emptiness out there. His hands gripped the railing. Never took much for him to slip through Nell's fingers. This morning it was the acrid stink of coal smoke from the *Etruria*'s stacks, a sudden clanging bell. She could see the haunting return. Hear the frantic whistling of the train. Hissing and screaming iron wheels screeching and sliding down the sloping grade of the track. Tom Thumb, shrieking, scooped up by the cowcatcher and tossed into a ditch. Jumbo, head swinging back defiantly, his last sound a roar as the locomotive struck with a deafening, sickening thud, derailing, riding over Jumbo as he collapsed, tearing his coarse hide into strips, the engineer leaping to safety under a rolling ball of fire as the iron horse tumbled down the embankment. And yet, Jumbo lived, mangled on the tracks, his great lungs labouring. Scotty clinging to his side, blackened by ash, begging the locusts that descended with pocketknives to clip souvenirs of ear and tufts of tail to have pity, for the love of God. Tom Thumb sprawling in a ditch, mewling in agony. Nell, torn, bruised, cut, crawling up the embankment through broken glass and sputtering lanterns, in time to see Jumbo's trunk, wrapped about his keeper, let go.

When Scotty's once-powerful hands, now thin and trembling, tightened around the ship's railing until they were white, Nell tugged the hem of his coat. Confused, he looked as if he didn't know her. Four years now since that ghastly night. Rocking and soothing him through grief-tormented dreams when she feared the drink would win. Stood between Scotty and Messrs. Hutchinson and Bailey, who were anxious to be done with a mournful face more suited to funerals than the circus. Battled her own demons that whispered, *Without Jumbo, he can be yours*. But occasionally there were small victories. Like today. Scotty had climbed up from the hold, where he bedded down between skin and bones in crates, and into morning where sea air put colour in his cheeks.

"Euna," he said, pulling the collar of his coat tight, words sounding unused to being spoken. "Pulled children around Three Island Pond in a cart. Ran onto the canal road like she wanted to get trampled by that carriage." Scotty glanced at Nell with a thin smile. "Don't know why I'm thinking about that now."

"Who was Euna?"

"An ostrich. Harness wore off all the feathers."

Always picking a bouquet of sorrows, that one, Dora told Nell. You think he knows any happy stories? Circus talk was, they'd be burying Scotty soon, not that anyone said it to Nell's face. Everyone knew she was the one pouring a bottle of whiskey into Scotty to get him standing—first one leg in his trousers, then the other, then the coat—only to prop him up in the ring, leading bones and hide and whining Alice, all the way from London. Circus folks were used to animals dying, so no one understood why Scotty was grieving so long after Jumbo being gone. Not manly, not manly at all. And after the Bridgeport fire, Scotty, also suffering the death of Alice, had to smear greasepaint over his skin so he didn't look yellow under the bright lights.

That Miss-In-Your-Business Dora could shut up as far as Nell was concerned, as if anything coming out of the back end of a cow was worth a listen. What did she know? Just you living with your crazy man, Dora might say, even laugh, if she knew what Nell was up to, instead of keeping her mouth shut. She'd find out they'd run away like everyone else, when curtains opened and no Scotty. No Nell. Served Dora right being stuck on that stinking cargo ship full of animals—and Elephant Bill—when she could have been using that extra bed in Nell's cabin, if she'd been a better friend and Nell had a mind to offer.

What Dora, being part cow, didn't see was people's faces when Nell and Scotty dragged skin and bones into the rings. Women and children near to tears, grown men chewing tobacco and looking at their feet, remembering days when Jumbo roared and stomped, and who cared if he really was the biggest elephant in the world. In that moment, everyone looking believed it. How much longer were they gonna buy tickets to a funeral march? To be made sad. Or even to see the tiniest woman in the world? She's seen the pamphlets. Do-gooders giving speeches in churches, saying modern times meant it was cruel paying to gawk at God's misfortunate. But goodness Heavens! Didn't want Nell sitting at their dinner tables or working for them. They just wanted to feel Christian-like, knowing people that should have got tossed back weren't making a living being stared at in a midway.

Sure, would leave Mr. Barnum in a fix if those righteous folks got their way. He'd have to find another mummified fish he could stitch into a mermaid. But Barnum was forgetting things now, taking those spells, having to sit and catch his breath. Maybe Mr. Hutchinson and Elephant Bill were good at making excuses for him, but Barnum could just as soon drop dead—and where would that leave Nell? Or any of them? Someone come along, buy up the circus. Find herself begging for bread caged next to a bear in some travelling freak show in the South. Be dead in a week in that heat. Less, if Elephant Bill...and if not him, plenty others like him.

That's why the more Nell got thinking about what she had to do, the more she was convinced London was Barnum's last hurrah, him stunning the crowd—no, the world—like he did, announcing Jumbo's triumphant return, accompanied by the full circus, words Scotty had long been desperate to hear. Only too late. Just might be her last hurrah, too, if everything worked out like she planned, feeling every dollar she could get her hands on stitched into her corset with that tore-out page from *David Copperfield.* Very sorry if the next person coming along to read the book needed the words on the other side of that picture of an upside-down boat turned into a house. Not that living on a beach gave Nell much comfort thinking about tides and storms, but with a little money saved, and maybe helped herself to, she could let a cottage somewhere. See the ocean every day. Her and Scotty.

So, Nell ignored what anyone thought, and didn't care if Scotty wanted to sleep rough between the two large Jumbos in crates, not in the steerage bunk Barnum had arranged for him. Or with her. But she made it her duty to get him on deck of the *Etruria* each morning, hiding her happy tears when seeing a somewhat healthier glow. And he was eating, just not enough to fill out his coat or hold up his trousers.

"How many more days?" he asked that morning.

A few more, Nell guessed, remembering her first voyage.

The mid-Atlantic was gentler today, but coal smoke still blew down across the deck and yanked at the open parasol in Nell's hand. No way was she closing it, not until those first-class ladies got eyes full of the exquisite blue roses stitched about the satin.

"Mr. Barnum took me to London when he brought me to the circus. Made a big to-do about showing me to the Queen. I didn't like her dog."

The first of many disappointments in her new life.

"She came to the zoo," said Scotty.

Along with a small regiment on horseback, pride in the memory of it, because of all the wonders of the world the London Zoological Society had on offer, Her Majesty cared nothing for chimpanzees in pinafores eating dinner in the Monkey House with a fork. Or mandrills and langurs. Not penguins, pink-headed ducks from the Sandwich Islands, Bengal tigers gifted from her empire in India, a cheetah, black African panther, Montezuma the Mexican jaguar, lynx from snow-white Hudson Bay, elands, a gnu, an oryx, and hartebeests.

Not even one of the rough-coated ponies rumoured to have sired a herd after being shipwrecked on a sandbar in the North Atlantic. No, sir. Jumbo, she said. Queen Victoria only wanted her children to ride on Jumbo.

Even so, her showing up like that, not right lowering the howdah onto Jumbo just so the prince and princess could have a private ride and then stay strapped on all day, especially so soon after being rattled by that man claiming Jumbo tried to step on him.

"Ah, blather, Miss Nell, but Jumbo getting so famous, that sort of trickery came about. I'd put my life against it that my Jumbo was innocent." The drip on the end of Scotty's nose got ready to drop. "Going on about compensation. Bartlett and Dr. Sclater told me they didn't care for this man going to the newspapers, giving the Society a bad name, said I'd keep the pennies from folks riding Jumbo if I helped them know what happened."

Nell glanced up at him from under her parasol.

"Found that sweet roll under the mulberries, full of fishhooks. Told them the man must have been trying to feed it to Jumbo."

If there was a moral crisis, it had long been resolved.

"Good. I'm glad you did it, Mr. Scott. For Jumbo."

The ship's stack rumbled and spewed a wad of black, oily smoke, startling a coterie of ladies up ahead, who then covered their mouths with gloved hands and laughed at their fright. Nell rested her hand on Scotty's forearm to steady him.

"So, what did she wear?"

"Who?"

"The Queen."

"Oh, her. Only saw the bottom of her dress through the carriage door, but the young prince paid me two pennies for the rides."

They took another turn around the deck, Nell clutching Scotty whenever the *Etruria* gently rolled, liking the feel of his arm.

"You'll see your family, in London?"

Scotty rubbed his hands together, gave them a shot of his breath.

"They'd be up at Knowsley, outside Liverpool. My brother took over brewing for the earl after my father died. Not a forgiving man."

Why was not offered.

No one else? Lady Muckety-Muck, whose name Nell convinced herself she couldn't remember, even if she did. She twirled her dazzling parasol and smiled at other passengers watching and pointing and no doubt wondering what to make of such an odd pair. Tittle-tattle over luncheon for sure. But Nell did remember that woman all right. Elinor. Gorgeously dressed Elinor. Lady Elinor. Begged to be hated.

A man nodded as he passed them on the deck. White hair, a cane. The woman by his side smiled benignly, the way a woman can when she knows dinner will be served to her when she walks through the door, and a hot bath ready before bed. "Your dear child looks exhausted," she noted to Scotty, not unkindly, but as once and always a mother. Then, lingering a moment or two longer and seeing all not being what it first appeared, her eyes widened, and she hurried the man away on the heels of a tiny gasp.

"I would like to see the zoo again," Scotty decided right then.

First time he'd wished it for Nell to hear. Jumbo and Alice swimming and spraying each other in Regent's Canal, even if the green water didn't look fit for bathing. Children scrambling for a look, toddlers on shoulders. Lads waving hats. *Huzzah! We love you, Jumbo! Give Alice a kiss for us! Hurrah for our dear wee Jumbo!* But he was just a calf back then. Then quiet walks through pathways woven into groves, by the nose-picking kid selling sweet rolls with his blind grandmother, buying the one Scotty needed to find under the mulberry tree with the fishhooks, trailed by that chatty niece of Bartlett's, heart of a lad, growing up fast. Pestering keepers, feeding parrots. No sitting around with silly girls pricking silly fingers, stitching silly samplers, giggling while rolling their hair in curling papers, and wondering if soldiers in tight trousers were marching in Hyde Park. No, that would never do for her.

Elinor.

A rogue wave splashed cold and wet over the promenade, scuttling passengers near the bow. Nell, not being one to hide from rough weather, dismissed the offer of shelter.

"You must know that Jumbo, as he is now, can't stay in the circus much longer. People don't want to see him like that." Scotty needed telling, needed hearing. "And then what will you do?"

"I made a promise, Miss Nell. See no reason not to keep it."

"Yes, but that was…before."

"Maybe…" His coat blown open, shirt stained with slop and sweat, thoughts in another time. "…Elinor could help."

Nell's grip on the handle of her parasol tightened.

"Her Ladyship now. Married Lord Leeston of Halfmoon Bay."

"And why would lady, whatever her name is, of Halfmoon Bay help you?"

Scotty pulled a flat brown bottle from inside his pocket, not a care about what pish-posh passengers scattering about the deck might think. Or what Nell did.

"She loved Jumbo too."

But there was more, much more.

"And?"

"She was…"

The girl who crawled out of her bedroom window because she wanted to be first to see baby Jumbo come from Paris; a girl who dreamed of being a veterinarian; how the hoops of her dress flipped sideways slipping into the den, boys' boots and pantalets for all to see. How big would Jumbo grow? What would Jumbo eat? Would his tusks be very long? Not even waiting for answers, driving Euna's cart because if boys could ride an ostrich, why not her? And when her uncle, the superintendent, demanded Scotty break Jumbo so children could ride, and if not him, then Godfrey—except he had a mean streak and head keeper Thompson had a missus and those young elephant bastards can run fast—it was light-as-a-feather Elinor who slipped gingerly onto his back. The first of much willfulness that would send her nervous aunt to recover near the lakes. And when the rhino gored Thompson, it was Elinor who scandalously tied off his torn leg, being alone in a place of men she shouldn't have been, getting herself forced into marriage with a fat widower as thanks. Much to forget, and yet…

"Were you and she—"

Scotty turned back to the sea. "Ah, leave be."

"Did you—"

But he cut her off, tossed his bottle and angrily reached for her, yanked the parasol out of her hand. Having smouldered from cinders falling from the ship's smokestacks, it burst into flame. Those on the promenade cheered and clapped as Scotty dropped it overboard.

KNOWSLEY

London, 1889

No cheering crowds greeted the lowering of the two giant crates onto Millwall Dock.

Why would they, they're coffins, thought Nell.

"Did Mr. Barnum forget to take out notices in the newspapers?" Scotty asked.

The old man might be getting forgetful, but not that forgetful. None of this bode well for Jumbo's "triumphant" return to London.

Only the occasional onlooker stopped to ponder wagons covered with Barnum circus posters slowly drawn through streets to West Kensington, where sombre rain pelted the barrel-vaulted roof of the Olympia. Home for the next three months.

Elephant Bill and the rest of the circus animals unloaded a few days later and followed in a caravan through the streets, Dora surprisingly congenial about forced travel with the animals. Told Nell she'd met a new man at sea, Charlie Dibbons, billed himself as Salazar and performed in a fetchingly cut coat. He travelled with six trained seals. One of them bit off most of his hand and he almost perished from blood poisoning, so he wore gloves and no one noticed the fake fingers.

"More than make do with the real ones," Dora was almost singing. "And you're just green with envy, setting your sights on a man who'd rather sleep with elephant bones."

When the Princess of Wales was profuse in her praise at seeing the new American show in the great exhibition hall, lines to buy tickets stretched into next week. Until the Jumbos rolled out under the glass vault. Scotty may have found comfort being back in London, but Nell saw only rows of disappointment. To many watching, some who'd ridden on Jumbo's back around the grounds of the zoo, sitting with their own children, there was nothing of the playful, cantankerous Children's Friend in Jumbo's skeleton and stuffed hide dragged on squeaking wheels. The end of Jumbomania came with polite, but short applause, and for Nell, fear.

Barnum, however, believed his usual force of optimism could alter his fortunes. He offered free admittance for the inhabitants of London's orphanages. Surely the delight of children would echo praise throughout the city. But by their sobbing at the sight of stuffed Jumbo slowly creaking around the Olympia, followed by Nell propping up Scotty reeking of drink, Barnum conceded defeat.

"In New York, we call these early performances 'previews,'" he announced jovially to the *Times* as if the disaster was according to plan. "To ready the circus for the real event, a spectacle the likes of which London, and dare I say all of England, has never seen before!"

Then he shuttered the return of Jumbo.

JUMBO'S BONES WERE ALREADY THE COLOUR OF HONEY. Bones and mounted hide were kept under canvas in the Olympia, where each morning during the circus hiatus, Scotty climbed a ladder with a wet cloth tied to a broom and polished. Made no sense to Nell. Taking care of something she loved was one thing, something she *had* loved, well, that was tomfoolery.

She dragged her portmanteau nearby, and on her knees, was pulling out burgundies and ochres and emeralds with cinched waists and leg-of-mutton sleeves. Nothing she owned even remotely resembled ancient Rome and that meant she'd have to make peace with Dora. She was the best seamstress in the circus, and if anyone could make Nell look like a Roman goddess, it'd be her. She carried on tossing silks and satins, Scotty up the ladder, and him, out of nowhere, standing there watching.

In well-worn Sunday best. Buttoned. Perhaps a bit too tight and fraying about the cuffs. Not a big man, but solid. Full beard flecked with grey, head not used to the hat. Standing somewhere between wonder and well put-upon.

"Matthew," he called, more like an order, as one not used to being ignored. "Come down from there."

Scotty stopped mid-wipe, the cloth at the end of the broom having come loose and fluttering to the bottom of the ladder. Then he climbed down, picked it up, and faced the older man. Nell could see it: recognition, the resemblance. Two old bulls. Neither offered a hand.

Scotty barely nodded.

"No words for me, brother?"

"Knowsley is a long way from London, Tom." Scotty, having spent decades commanding the largest animal in the world, spoke as one about to kneel.

"The train from Liverpool has much improved." Then Thomas nodded to Nell, confusion mixed with revulsion. "Who's *that*?"

While Nell wished the ground would open so she could crawl away, the awkwardness was ignored.

"Why are you here?"

"Read in the newspapers about your coming back with the great...Jumbo." Voiced with ridicule, as if stuffed hide with glass eyes, a skeleton, and wide-eyed Nell, whatever she was, with dark blue bombazine in hand, were hardly worth the price of admission, let alone the journey. "Came to see for myself."

"Disappointed?" Scotty started back up the ladder, but Thomas swung him around.

"Look at me, Matthew. Are you drinking?"

"Let me be, brother."

"I can smell it on you now, and you could barely stand out there, stumbling around after that monstrosity—"

Nell wasn't sure if the man meant her or the Jumbos.

"Thank Christ our mother didn't live to know what you've become, not that you cared. Left this world only wanting to see you one more time, and you couldn't be bothered."

"Animals don't stop being needed just because someone dies."

Like Alice did when the letter about Scotty's mother came. Her inexperienced keeper, young fool, tying her in for the night by her trunk. Silly animal took fright during a thunderstorm and tore a foot off the end. Days of cold-water baths before Scotty stopped the bleeding. Or Jumbo, rats devouring his feet and Scotty giving up his bed, armed with lantern and club to do battle all night long. And when Jumbo tried breaking out of his den and snapped off both his tusks, his face bloated with pus and he near died. Even Bartlett admitted only Scotty could lance those abscesses without getting killed. So why would Scotty leave for his mother's deathbed when she'd already be gone by the time he was by her side?

"Still as soft as that old earl was about these creatures." Thomas pulled off his hat like wearing it was a fashion he'd never quite understand. "It's him I blame, for this affectation of yours."

Scotty picked up his wash bucket. "It's you started it, making me crawl through his bird cages when I was a lad."

"We don't say no to the Earl of Derby. Everything we have is from his lot. You were old enough to earn your keep, but I never thought—"

Sloshing soapy water spilt between them. "His Lordship was a good, kind man. You'll not say otherwise to me. Sat by my bed every day, waiting for my leg to knit proper. And it never did, Tom."

"Ah, you would bring that up! Never should have happened. You know I was vexed—meant nothing by it, except teaching you a lesson."

Scotty might be a drunk, but long time since he was an obedient younger brother. "With a club?"

"He was a lord, for the love of Christ! And you, you're the son of a brewmaster. The two of you, carrying on over that menagerie of his while I had to take over, our father dead, our family to feed. You think I wanted that? You needed to remember your place." The brother thrust his finger angrily at Nell, as if the whole time, her presence had been an irritant. "And what is *she* doing here?"

Nell carefully placed her dresses in the portmanteau, closed it, and sat on top. No way was she missing out on old scores getting settled. Folded her arms just in case Scotty's brother needed clarity about her going nowhere.

"You sent me to London, Tom. I didn't want to go, I begged you to keep me, but you wouldn't even come to the station."

"Blame His Lordship if you must." Thomas trailed Scotty around, back to the ladder. "You and those bloody antelopes of his. It was him that arranged for you to take them to the zoo when he died."

"And I hated you both. Seventeen years old and given away like an animal. But you know, took me a long time to realize that man was more a father to me than my own. Sending me to London was his gift."

Thomas beat his chest. "*I* was a father to you!"

"No, Tom. Much, but never that."

Old words going round and round. Scotty climbed back up the ladder to Jumbo's bones, his brother a festering boil below.

"All right, Matthew. Let's leave the past. Come home. There's work, real work, and from the looks of you, Sunday prayer wouldn't go amiss either. Give up this foolhardiness. The circus is no place for a God-fearing man. I won't have our name laughed over in the newspapers."

Scotty glanced down at his brother. "Ah, so that's it. You're ashamed of my being in the circus."

"Turning yourself into one of these freaks." Thomas glanced at Nell cautiously, quickly, as if eye contact might infect future progeny. "And why is *she* here?"

Scotty nodded at Nell. "She's with me."

"*With*?"

And in the unbroken silence that followed, in that place of canvas and hide and bone, as sacred to Scotty as any cathedral, and before brothers parted unreconciled, Nell wondered at who her man had been before he was so broken.

THE DESTRUCTION OF ROME

The Olympia, 1889

If Nell moved again, she'd look more like a Roman whore than goddess, and a bloody one at that. Dora was stitching the filmy costume she was fitting, and it made no sense to her why Nell was jerking about, reading through newspaper advertisements for a cottage to let. In less than three months, they'd be sailing back to New York City. Dora had to shout above the hammering to be heard.

The orchestra rehearsing that new piece by the composer from Milan was a cacophony of crashing cymbals and horns. Screeching cats, thought Nell with a headache. Limber dancers held one leg over their heads and hopped about on the other. Men with ropes and pulleys crawled over a vast stage, carrying bits of wooden columns and temples, arches, *trompe l'oeil* yews, and blue sky and clouds painted on boards. Someone was always yelling: *Where are they? No! No! No! Higher! Higher!*

When P. T. Barnum's re-envisioned spectacle, The Destruction of Rome, or The Dawn of Christianity, opened, a procession of camels and white horses ridden by turbaned Arabs and elephants draped in embroidery led an army of twirling barely clothed nimbly dancing girls. Marching bands followed, men in white wigs wearing togas, servants carrying braised peacock and stuffed pig and baby lamb fashioned from papier mâché and garnished on silver trays. Half-naked slaves bent under chests of glass painted in gold and ruby. Swarthy gladiators bronzed with oil and criss-crossed with chains and wielding swords, barking dogs, flag bearers, squealing pigs and snarling lions led a pantheon of gods and goddesses pulled in chariots, rows and rows of undulating gold and indigo and crimson shimmering silk, barefoot vestal virgins tossing rose petals as they circled and danced, and a slow-moving Jumbo, wheeled by sweating Egyptian slaves, kept in sync by the beat of a drum.

Nero followed in a litter, carried onto the stage and, with one wave of his fat hand and trumpeting horns dripping red velvet, ignited the Olympian games. Chariots raced without rules about the perimeter, gladiator swords clanging in fight-to-the-death battles, parading lions and tigers and the snap of whips and snarls and roars, parted by a full-sized replica of a Roman ship rolling across the sand, escorted by jumping wooden dolphins, one hundred oars pulled in unison, deck urns on fire, exploding fireworks, and underworld demons writhing in belief-defying contortions.

For days before the show opened, Nell pleaded with Barnum for the role of the virtuous Christian beauty who enters after the barbarians swarm the Olympia, carry women off over their shoulders, and sack Rome.

"Boys," he laughed to the ones in tow, "our Miss Nell wants to play our virgin and I say ho ho!"

Much laughter heralded agreement.

Instead, she was dressed as a goddess and tied into a chariot so she wouldn't fall out, driven by two men blackened with boot polish to resemble Nubians. When asked what goddess she was portraying, no one knew, or cared. Those bloody Romans had so many. On her dizzying flights about the ring, she watched ushers carry out spectators overcome by spectacle. Or perhaps by the lack of clothing. Dozens every performance. She pretended to throw a lightning bolt made from balsa wood into an audience cheering so wildly, no one could hear the music and everyone was always missing cues.

At the end of each rapturous—and sold-out—fall of Rome, Barnum, white-haired and resplendent in princely garb, entered the Olympia in a carriage pulled by six horses for three celebratory rides about the rings, waved on by a sea of handkerchiefs while bloody sand was raked over, and dead and dying animals and a keeper, crushed by two elephants having enough of Hannibal Bill trekking through the Alps, were tossed into the backs of wagons. Applause was deafening; blinding joy beaming from Barnum's face. The great showman had not lost his magic touch. His last turn each night under the glare of lights was always the slowest, and Nell, who knew much of him, sensed indeed, farewell.

WHEN THE CHARIOT STOPPED, NELL TIED HER ROBES ABOUT HER knees. Those fellows playing barbarians out there really were barbarians, spitting out streams black with tobacco juices, didn't matter that some of the dancers had bare feet, mucking up shit and splashing about piss from hundreds of over-ridden and terrified animals. Soiled white hems on a goddess just wouldn't do.

Climbing down by the tented enclosure to the Jumbos, Nell watched a woman pushing her way through the canvas flaps. Recognized her instantly. No scallop stitching trimmed with wiggling tassels this time, no velvet cuffs about her wrists. All black. Except for the frothy cream jabot of lace tumbling down her front. In mourning, thought Nell, just not broken up over it.

"...in the newspapers what happened with the train. How sad he looks now," the woman was saying. "When I last saw him in New York—"

Elinor. Damn her.

The steady march of horses and camels and elephants as they lumbered and squawked and jingled out of the Olympia made Nell miss every other word she tried to overhear, hidden as she was.

"You were there?"

"My late husband had business. I accompanied him. Did that... not give you my note?"

Nell thought she heard Elinor call her a *creature,* but with the ruckus, she couldn't be sure.

"And you, Mr. Scott? You look unwell."

Nell could smell the whiskey even from behind the canvas.

"No...no, but as you can see, very demanding."

"Yes, a great success. Everyone in London pleads for tickets."

Dora, wearing a dolphin on her front and back, tied with leather straps that moved when she walked, hissed at Nell, demanded to know what she was up to.

"Get along," she hissed back, but only with wide eyes and flapping hands.

"...I thought you might have forgotten me," Elinor was saying, again about that visit in New York City.

"No, not forgotten. I could never forget you, Elinor." Her name on his lips sounded like it might have once been *his* Elinor.

"Between us now, it can only be Lady Leeston and Mr. Scott."

Nell exhaled, hadn't realized she'd been holding her breath.

"I must go."

"So soon?"

"My aunt and uncle will be waiting."

"Bartlett?"

"The superintendent to you, Mr. Scott."

"Yes, of course."

Nell gathered from rustling muslin that the audience was ending.

"But...you haven't seen Jumbo. Not properly."

"Goodbye, Mr. Scott."

"Wait—"

*No...no...*Nell wanted to scream over Scotty's hasty and rough words of regret and desire, but bit into her hand.

"My dear Mr. Scott. We were very young then. Now it is I who must refuse you."

In the lengthy silence that followed, Nell imagined Elinor looking up into Jumbo's glass eyes as what remained of her first love collapsed in front of her. And maybe that's what Her Ladyship had really wanted all along. Nell hated this woman, but thanked her, for there could be no hope now and Scotty must know. And when Elinor exited the tent, she passed Nell without even noticing.

LONG LIVE THE KING

London Zoological Gardens, 1890

The carriage driver up top stomped his foot. "South entrance to the London Zoo, Broad Walk, mate." Deserted, save for a slouching attendant, guarded by spikes of cast iron, towered over by leafless beech.

Scotty pulled down the carriage window. January dull and cold eagerly rushed in. Nell watched memory and grief play out on his face. Twenty years before, he and a diseased elephant calf, no bigger than a large dog, tracking bloody footprints all the way from Waterloo station in coal fog so thick they coughed up orange spit, entered their life here together. Jumbo's rat-eaten feet wrapped in Scotty's shirts and chased by boys pelting them with rotten tomatoes.

The driver wanted to know, was the fare and his young miss getting out, or heading back to Kensington? He left them, to the sound of wheels and hooves clattering away on the cobbles, dry and curled leaves somersaulting across the walk.

Scotty tightened his scarf. Not the homecoming he'd dreamed.

But it was Nell who faltered at the gate, trembling fingers slipping into Scotty's calloused hand, not because of her hopes, but because of winter murmuring in the branches overhead and distant impotent roars, frantic fluttering, and ceaseless chirping. Animal fear in this place like a stink. Wandering, leaf-strewn avenues where despair and children petted the weak and waved sweet cakes before the chained and starving, indulgent parents smiling wanly at animals and birds poked in tiny cages, circling or flapping or pacing, endlessly… endlessly. A pitiful life. Her life. Scotty, clutching for a foothold in a changed landscape. Nell disguised as a child. No one clamouring to see P. T. Barnum's biggest star and Jumbo's former keeper.

"Elinor wore a sash like that when she was your age." Scotty couldn't be sure; it was, after all, years ago. Nell was only pretending to be that young, and he kept glancing back towards an alehouse he was sure used to be on Albany Street. "Or was it yellow. Yes, I think so, on a dress with little blue flowers on it. She'd stuff it with crab-apples, for Jumbo."

The past brought no pleasure in telling or hearing.

"It was her that named Jumbo. Bloody French, couldn't even bother to give him a name. *Jeunes-beaux! Jeunes-beaux!* is all I got when I asked. Imagine calling that poor sickly thing young and beautiful. I'm telling you, those French haven't got the sense the good Lord gave them. Looking at him? No one expected him to live a week. And Bartlett, fool wanted to name him Horatio, you know, to honour our great war hero, Nelson. But after Elinor said, *Jum-bo*..."

"I don't want to go."

Nell had rehearsed the words like a new song for the Hippodrome, except no clowns or jugglers or trapeze artists, or thousands of spectators watching every godawful moment. Only Scotty, broken, here before her. Now or never. Buried things should stay buried. Here, the zoo. Elinor. Even Jumbo. Ahead? Nothing except life, their life, what was left; surely she could make him understand now.

"I don't want to go in there," she said again.

Not to the zoo, not back to the Olympia, not even to New York City, not anywhere without him. Of course, Scotty didn't love her, not like Jumbo, not even that Elinor; maybe never would, maybe incapable of it, or he might come to one day. Didn't matter. No need to live as man and wife. Who needs the full slice of dream when a sliver will do? She'd found a cottage overlooking the sea, in Bournemouth, away from where people might think them strange. What little money she'd cobbled together spent to let it. For them. Nell would make bread, she was sure she'd be good at it given a chance, her own kitchen, warm and welcoming, and have a table in a parlour with a crystal vase. She always wanted to have a crystal vase, filled with hydrangea grown in a garden. Their garden. No freaks, no circus, no elephants. *No Jumbo.* Wouldn't even tell Dora because she'd just be jealous, and oh, wouldn't Nell love that. This was her chance. Her one chance to be normal.

Timidly, she tugged at his fingers. "Mr. Scott…Scotty—"

But his faraway gaze was for gaslights glowing on the Outer Circle road. "Look at the hour, best get back." Hard sounding, as if chastising a naughty child, and pulled his hand free.

NELL SAT ON HER BUNK WATCHING DORA UNPACK HER TRUNK. A blanket hung from a rope strung between the two beds was gently swinging back and forth. If ever Nell wanted to know what getting her head bashed in with a stone felt like, she'd remember this day.

"Zebras tried to get away when the ship was loading in New York City," Nell whispered, still wearing her hat and gloves.

"Heard that."

"Bill shot them."

"Heard that too," replied Dora. "Why you grieving about that now?"

They were lucky.

Nell closed her eyes, lay back, and looked up. Nine plus nine was eighteen. Old. Plus nine was twenty-seven. Older. Plus nine was thirty-six. Ancient.

Dora pulled back the blanket curtain.

"Not that I told you so, Nell, but I told you so. Maybe you'll listen to me now about getting a real man, like my Charlie."

"You're not bringing that one-handed seal trainer in here."

"Cheer up. Circus won't be needing your *unmovable* Mr. Scott when we get home, and then he'll be out of your hair. Get a second chance, if you're smart."

Nell sat up. "What do you mean?"

"I heard Jumbo's going to a museum." Dora pulled a frock from one of the drawers in her trunk and held it up. "You'll be next. Mark my words."

"You're lying. Mr. Barnum would never part with Jumbo."

"Alive? No. But that sad pile of skin and bones? Now, don't you be freezing me, Nell. Charlie told me. Swears it's true. On my heart. Cost Mr. Barnum a fortune bringing him here, not that the English much care about him being back. Guess a telegram's already been sent to Mr. Bailey about making it happen.

"Hey—" Dora ran after Nell into the passageway. "Where're you going?"

"To find out if this is true."

"The hold? It's not safe down there. Nell—"

She walked unsteadily—hallways, stairs, decks swaying as the ship laboured in rough seas. Scotty'd never said a word. He couldn't know. Be like Barnum, let a man go with no warning. Or her. Not that Nell couldn't see it coming. Should have seen it coming. Dead Jumbo was sad Jumbo. She'd tried to warn Scotty. At least there was still time. What remained for either of them in America now?

The hallways narrowed. Third class was less fancy than second. Steerage plain, but freshly painted. Going from bitter disappointment back to high hopes took some doing without getting lightheaded. No museum was going to let Scotty follow around what was left of Jumbo, he'd have to know that. She'd tell him. The ship made its last call at Portsmouth before crossing the Atlantic. Why not disembark?

With the door to the hold closing behind her, the brightly lit passageway darkened with low flickering lamps. The metal stairs descended to a landing, turned, and vanished into gloom. Cages crammed in, elephants, horses, camels, lions. The gagging stench of confinement. Roars and grunts and howls and yelps—animals, terrified and confused by constant near darkness, the rocking of the ship, the endless pulse and throb from the steam engines. The floor of the hold shimmered with a piss river of running shit, piles of straw doing nothing to soak it up.

Scotty was not far. The crates containing Jumbo's remains were buttressed against the hull. No berth for him. He'd be rolled out beside them, probably with a pipe already on the go.

But maybe Dora was right. The hold was darker than she expected. Maybe best to go back and find a steward. And Nell would've, except grabbing hold of bars to something, her hand was licked. Gasping, she yanked it away and almost toppled onto the glistening floor. The roaring stopped her. Of all the animal noises down here, this wasn't fear. No, this was rage. Torment. The clink of metal against metal. And then, that hearty laugh. A man's laugh. That man. She knew it, and who'd made it. Sucked the beating heart from her. Behind her, the stairs. Ahead, equal distance to where she'd find Scotty. Safe. Between both, down the narrow corridor of skittish mules in cages, Elephant Bill, jabbing the long blunt end of his bullhook into King Mykonos's cage, the enraged gorilla fighting off the blows.

Nell covered her mouth but not fast enough.

"Who's there?"

Every day for months, thousands watching in the Olympia, and if not them, Scotty by her side. Never alone. She'd let herself ignore the fear of him, even though he was somewhere, everywhere. And now she'd foolishly walked right to him. How could she be so stupid?

"Mr. Scott!" Nell called.

Elephant Bill wrestled the bullhook out of the gorilla's hands and tossed it at his feet.

"Little Eyes? Is that you come sneaking around to see me?"

"Mr. Scott!"

"Gotta scream louder than that, little one. He's long into his bottle."

Nell ran for the stairs but slipped in slick urine and feces. Elephant Bill laughed heartily, watching her grabbing hold of cages.

"Now there, Nell, you hurt my feelings. We've got lots to talk about, you playing hard at getting reacquainted. Maybe later for talking, that is. It's this you're after, eh?" He cupped his groin. "They all say no, but like you, they come back for more."

"You leave me be, Bill!"

He shook his head. "Missed your charms, Nell. Been a long, long time."

She held the bars tight, wished she could be locked inside with the mule staring back with empty eyes, probably thinking for once it was glad to be in a cage. Rows of them between her and Bill, but she could already imagine the lick of his tongue, his fingers, him shoving up inside her, holding her neck tight while her crying made no sound at all.

"I'll scream!"

"Above all these animals? No one's going to come."

And the ship lurched, the bullhook Bill had tossed went underfoot. When he stepped towards her, the bullhook slipped out and he fell back against the gorilla's cage. Not enough to injure, but enough for the ever-watching, ever-waiting, ever-vengeful King Mykonos to slide his hands through the bars, wrap them around Elephant Bill's chest.

Now it was Bill's turn to roar, as if a command from him would cause the long-tormented gorilla to obey. But King Mykonos held firm. When Bill tried to reach the metal prod with his foot, the gorilla yanked him up until he dangled above the floor. His cry was like a screech. The gorilla slammed him down, Bill dazed, his head rolling. Great, hairy hands moved down Bill's chest, snapping each set of ribs as he pressed, Bill gurgling, whatever he had for dinner bubbling up like a cool spring fountain. The gorilla pulled Bill's arms back through the bars of the cage, tearing them out of each socket, then bone breaching skin.

Nell's wet skirts clung to her as she slowly pulled herself up.

"Help me...help me...for the love of Christ...Nell, help..."

King Mykonos looked at her and grunted. Lifted Elephant Bill again and pulled one of his legs through the bars.

Snap.

"Nell...for God's sake..."

She'd always known Elephant Bill was fearsome; she hadn't reckoned he was this tough. To still be alive, to still be conscious. To still feel this kind of pain.

The gorilla had pressed what he could of his face through the bars and panted into Bill's ear. Nell would never forget that man's look, not that she'd ever want to. Knowing he was going to die, but not yet, not for a while. And Nell, taking a seat on a crate, was going to witness every slow, agonizing minute. The last sound he made, a yelp, was when his trousers darkened. Bill was right. No one heard the screams.

WHEN NELL STEPPED BACK INTO THE WELL-LIT PASSAGEWAY, she leaned against the wall.

In.

Out.

Deep breaths.

The stink of the hold saturating her clothes. Maybe even murder, what she'd done. She didn't care. Joy she didn't think possible rose up from someplace she didn't know existed. *Ha!* Free. And not just free, but like she could stretch out her hands and calm the very seas.

This is what it must feel like to walk through the world as normal.

This is what it must feel like to be a man.

WE SHALL NOT SPEAK OF THIS AGAIN

London, 1890

When Nell, every resplendent inch billed to P. T. Barnum's account, walked into the Hotel Victoria near Charing Cross, she blew two-handed kisses to the guests in the lobby who'd stopped mid-sentence to gawk. She demanded a room, preferably not overlooking the noisy boulevard. Barnum and his wife were staying at the hotel because Nancy had been ill, which had delayed them sailing with the rest of the circus.

She's always sick, that one, Dora once said, but if that kept an eighty-year-old man from creeping into your bed, she'd claim to have the scoots and be puking all day too.

Nell, unannounced, found Barnum in his suite, behind a large walnut desk, surrounded by his usual young, fashionable men. Only these eager fellows spoke with English accents and various degrees of concern.

"Little Eyes?" Barnum's hands silenced the room. "Why are you not on your way to New York?"

The train of Nell's dress dragged on a carpet swirling with crimson roses. She glared at the young man sitting in the chair across from Barnum who searched faces for a cue as to what he should do, then sheepishly offered her the seat.

"I changed my plans."

The row of young men in stripes and grey appeared too startled by her to even blink.

"As you say, then, why don't you visit Mrs. Barnum. She's resting at the moment, but I'm sure—"

"It's you I've come to see, and I will do."

"Yes, but my dear, you must excuse us. I've just received some dreadful news. Terrible, terrible. There's been an accident—"

"Yes?"

"On the ship, the one you're supposed to be on."

Nell folded her leather-gloved hands and looked about at everyone. Barnum and the others seemed perplexed by her unwillingness to avoid the indelicacy.

"I don't know how to say this, but our beloved Elephant Bill's been lost."

"How horrible." She smiled placidly.

"Yes...yes, an accident in the hold. One of the animal crates was not secured, the poor man was crushed."

"Indeed dreadful," agreed Nell.

"His wife will have to be told, arrangements made." Barnum's brow furrowed as if the idea had just come to him and was potentially costly.

"She'll be devastated, I'm sure."

One of the young men standing wrote furiously and kept looking towards the door, but Nell had no intention of leaving. The murmuring and nodding men reminded her of pigeons.

"Perhaps we could meet for tea in a day or so when Mrs. Barnum is well. I'm quite fond of English tea—"

"This won't wait. I have an appointment with a reporter from the *Times* in one hour."

The showman held his ground, but the boys faltered, looking awkwardly at each other or out windows.

"Lads, excuse us. Little Eyes is, after all, my biggest attraction, and has come all this way." Then he looked at Nell coldly. "It must be very important to interrupt me so."

When the boys in suits rolled and tumbled out of the hotel room, Barnum put on his displeased face, lurched forward, but before he could demand to know what she wanted in as condescending a manner as possible, Nell rose majestically:

"I'm leaving the circus," she said. *Boom. Right between the eyes.*

"What? Why? You can't—"

"Okay then, I've left the circus."

"Good heavens, Miss Nell, my dear Little Eyes, what's gotten into you?" The old man sat back hard as if winded.

"I want my life."

"Impossible."

"I don't need," she slowly pulled off her gloves, one finger at a time, "your permission."

"A woman like *you*? You can't be out in the world. It will devour you. Now what's brought this on, my dear? To say such hurtful words to me? I've been your family since you were a child. I've given you everything, my circus has given you everything. The very clothes on your back. And… protected you."

"Yes, a walking sandwich board for the Greatest Show on Earth everywhere I go."

"Ridiculous. No, hysterical. Whatever it is that ails you, calm yourself. Shall I send for the hotel doctor?"

"I'm perfectly calm, as you can see, Mr. Barnum."

"And we do have a contract." Ah, there it was, as expected.

"The one you signed with my mother. Dead mother."

Barnum folded his hands over his waistcoat and length of silver. Showed no emotion. Tough negotiations were nothing new.

"All right then, why are you really not on your way to New York?"

"I want a hundred thousand dollars."

"Is that so?" Barnum chuckled. "Whatever for?"

"I've done my sums. Partly for the money owed me for being your trick pony all these years."

"Absurd. I owe you nothing."

"The rest is compensation. For Jumbo."

"Jumbo? Ah, I see...of course. That's what this is all about. Is our Mr. Scott behind you being here? Is what they say about you and him true? I heard tell about your relations and I must say I've been very tolerant—"

"He knows nothing."

"You've heard then, I'm retiring Jumbo from the show?"

"Dead Jumbo," said Nell.

"Yes, very tragic, how can we forget."

"I can't, I was there. Or that you killed him."

The nerve skewered, the great showman circled the desk, pulling himself around the edge by his hands, towered over her, face as red as the roses on the carpet.

"Mind what you say. Even my generosity has limits."

"You knew he was sick, you knew he was dying, and instead of sending Jumbo back to Bridgeport where maybe, just maybe, he might have had a chance, you had Elephant Bill kill him. Too bad that lawsuit against the railroad didn't work out, or you'd have come out of this quite handsomely."

"Shame on you, you vile creature—and that great man not cold in his grave. You've always hated Bill, made up those horrible stories about him. You lied to me then, Nell, and you're lying to me now."

"Am I? Bill never showed an animal a moment of kindness until that night when he arranged to have the fence taken down so poor Jumbo wouldn't have far to walk. On tracks where he knew a train was coming. Or that man, Ward? The very man you arranged to skin Jumbo's hide when his blood was still flowing. To get to St. Thomas when he did, he must have left days before Jumbo's final performance."

"You're mad, Nell. Besotted with that Englishman." Yelling, hands trembling threateningly, inches from her face, each promise of retribution an octave higher. "I've given you a wonderful life, you should be thankful, not blackmailing me. Not one penny will you get!"

He raised his fist as if to smite an Old Testament foe back into submission, but Nell, amused, shrugged ever so slightly.

"You're afraid," she said, and loved every second of it.

Her coldness was unnerving, and Barnum, baffled at feeling rebuked, stumbled back to let her pass, her train dragging behind her.

"As I said, I'll be speaking to the *London Times.* And every other newspaper who'll listen."

Barnum ran before her, threw himself against the door with all the aplomb of a circus impresario done wrong, arms outstretched.

"Really, Mr. Barnum? Am I not the ingenue here?"

"No one will believe a circus freak." Nor would he end his blockade. "Did you want to see Jumbo suffer, is that it? He was dying and I did Scott and that animal a kindness by putting him down. The show goes on. That's all that matters."

"I'm not sure your adoring public will see it that way. The great Phineas Taylor Barnum. A lifetime bringing joy to people, and this is how they'll remember you. A liar. The man who killed Jumbo, the Children's Friend."

"This is how you repay me?" He was trembling now, spittle flying when he spoke.

Nell reached for the doorknob. "A bank draft to my room before the end of the day. For it, I'll never speak of what you've done. Or see you again."

And Barnum, speechless for once, stepped aside.

ACT VII

BACK TO THE BEGINNING

Medford, 1891

Because of the sloping roof Nell was the only one who could fully stand, but at least the damp stains blended into the faded pink geraniums on the wallpaper.

"Does the fireplace work?"

"Carrying up coal is extra." Mrs. Meck was hard with her words, as if anyone should doubt them.

Generously proportioned, with a penchant for floral prints, she was mistress of the rooming house on Custom Street, a lanky building held generously upright by its sturdy neighbours.

"Don't normally let this floor. Like I said, wish you'd let me show you the room downstairs. The gentleman would be more comfortable."

She joined Nell behind Scotty in a wicker chair. The window he looked out was set low in the gable.

"I'll grant you, best view in the house up here if you don't mind looking at fields. Nothing but snow in winter. That's Tufts College, up on the hill." Workmen on ladders were mortaring stone in the entranceway. "Took that door apart getting an elephant inside. Imagine that. Something to do with that circus fella dying, museum I expect. You hear about it? It was in all the newspapers. Rich men, always wanting to remind us they were here after they're gone."

Nell put her hand on Scotty's shoulder, felt him trembling, but not from the cold.

"It's perfect." He coughed, patted her hand.

"When is the room available?"

"The gentleman can stay now if you pay."

Nell followed Mrs. Meck onto the landing, closing the door behind her. She reached into the cloth bag secured to her wrist, counted out six months in advance, and the coal. The landlady watched hungrily.

"But I got a right to know what ails the man. He got something catchy?"

"He's been living rough."

"Ah, the drink is it?"

Nell nodded, but angrily.

"Thought so. Smell it on him."

"Mr. Scott is not one for socializing, so you'll see that he gets his meals?" Nell nodded to the money in hand. "I'm sure you'll find my settling of account satisfactory."

"Now don't you worry, miss…madam…miss. Local minister calls me an Angel of Mercy. You'll come by regular?"

"Not for some time. I…I must travel."

"If you don't mind me asking," said the landlady, shoes clattering on wooden steps as she hurriedly followed Nell down the narrow, uneven stairs and onto the porch where the carriage waited, "you ever thought about being in the circus?"

"No," replied Nell blankly. "Why would I?"

HAMBURG DELIGHTED NELL, PARTLY BECAUSE SHE COULDN'T understand a word, so if she was being talked about, she never knew, and for the most part, Germans didn't give her a second glance.

She found an undiscerning dressmaker around the corner from her hotel and, although brusque and indignant whenever Nell made a suggestion, she created a stunning walking dress and evening gown. The walking dress had a sky-blue jacket and was trimmed with black piping. Nell knew she'd never wear the silk ball gown but just having such splendour wrapped in rice paper and tucked in a box meant she could pretend.

The hotel also served an admirable whiskey in the private salon, of which Nell partook, getting tingly in the arse as Dora crudely put it, waiting to be audacious. She poured herself another as the doors to the salon slid open.

The man escorted in looked quizzically behind at the hotel clerk who was already on his way out.

Tall and thin, the middle-aged man had white hair, not from age, but from adventure, and grew a wild fringe down one side of his face, under the chin, and up the other side. And he stared.

"Yes, I'm quite small. Always good to get that out of the way, don't you think? Whiskey?"

"I…was to meet Herr Scott, from America."

Nell gestured to the chair across the table. "Do sit, Mr. Hagenbeck, I must apologize."

"I don't understand. Have we met…madam?" The English solid, the accent thick.

Nell sipped. "No, but I know you."

From that lavish celebration to christen the new Elephant House in the London Zoo, back in 1870, where Scotty may have only watched from the dens with Jumbo and Alice, while famed African hunter and honoured guest Carl Hagenbeck was lionized, but Scotty remembered well. Britannia on lamp poles. Children waving and spilling lemonade, faces dusted with sugar. Elephants, rhinos, a tapir paraded to their new home. Society members dining in the long visitors' gallery on ornamental carpets under paper lanterns, where swift-footed boys served covered plates run over from the Refreshment House: turtle soup, cakes in Madeira, and a jelly dusted with the ivory from a dead walrus. With heroic gestures and pulling imaginary triggers, Hagenbeck thrilled with Red Sea voyages, sands of the pharaohs, bandits, and naked horsemen. Sacrifices too great to speak of in front of the ladies and privation no other Christian man had endured—bringing the likes of Jumbo and Alice to the civilized world from the wilds of Sudan, where despite the splendid dinner,

Hagenbeck was relieved to see no elephant on the menu. A reference to war-besieged Paris, where starving citizens stormed the Jardin des Plantes to eat their beloved Castor and Pollux. *Here! Here!*

Yes, Carl Hagenbeck was the right man for Nell. From the papers on the table in front of her, she slid an envelope towards him.

The German recognized the handwriting. "How did you get that?"

"Really, the whiskey is very good, some of the best I've tasted. Come, let me pour you a glass. Or do Germans not drink whiskey?"

Hagenbeck, uncomprehending, very slowly lay his hat on the table.

"Your letters to Matthew Scott." Nell smiled demurely and unapologetically. "Would you have replied to a woman?"

"What game is this?"

Nell unfolded the bank draft for £5,000. "You are the animal dealer who brought Alice to the London Zoo, and as a young man, you followed the hunters who captured Jumbo."

The animal dealer's eyes widened at the draft, the great deal of money, and the glass of whiskey, and appeared to be unable to make sense of anything.

"Now, you must take *me* to Sudan."

"Not Herr Scott?"

"As you agreed. Half now, half when we return."

"*Nein, nein*...a woman? Small, like you? The danger, but why?"

"Enough for you to know that Mr. Scott cannot travel and is, perhaps, without much time. I want to help him keep a promise."

"And what promise is that?"

Penance at the River Royan, but that was only for Nell to know.

"I'm sorry, miss...madam. You don't know what you ask."

But, it was a great deal of money and business is business. Hagenbeck downed the whiskey with military precision.

Nell poured another.

"The hardships for a man on such a journey. But a woman—"

"Yes, yes, like me."

"I cannot guarantee your virtue."

"I'm not asking you to."

"The men I will need, how—"

"No one will know you travel with a woman."

Five thousand pounds, as expected, was impossible to refuse. As was the whiskey.

"One condition, Mr. Hagenbeck. You do not capture any animals on this trip."

The whiskey downed quickly; the glass hammered the tabletop in disbelief. "*Wahnsinn!* We can profit from the journey. The zoos, the circuses will pay what we ask."

"Not a single creature."

"To that godless land? Risk death? For nothing?"

Nell slid off her chair on her way to the door. "Enough has been taken," she said without looking back.

THE RED SEA

Egypt, 1892

The sky over the courtyard was blue. Dazzling, Egyptian blue. Mosaic pathways and trimmed grass meandered through the shading palms of the Suez Hotel. Past the pond and fountain gushing cool that looked a much older Ptolemaic than the hotel around it, walked the boy. Jodhpurs, double-breasted tunic, and cap. He wiped sweat climbing into the seat across from the animal hunter amid the potted fig trees.

"Remarkable," Hagenbeck observed. "No one would know."

"But wool, it's very hot," replied Nell.

"You'll be glad your skin is covered." Hagenbeck filled another glass and slid it towards her. "Sun here will bleach you to the bones in days. But, I think our Arab friends can help with a few modifications, to keep you cooler."

The potent liquor tasted of licorice.

"You do not care for it?"

"I'm supposed to be your young nephew. Should I not play the part?"

Hagenbeck gave her a dismissive snort, the kind Nell had come to expect as distinctively German. A short burst of air delivered with equal measures of ridicule and ennui. She was sure their language had a word for it.

"*Meine Dame,*" he said exaggeratedly, "you are in Suez, and besides, camel's milk is an acquired taste. Another?"

The heat from the liquor did somehow make her feel cooler.

Hagenbeck emptied his glass and gestured about the courtyard.

"Look around. Tomorrow, we begin our trek to Jumbo's home, from where his journey ended."

"Jumbo was here?"

"Tied to that very palm, with just enough rope to wade into the pond and eat the blue lotuses. Rare, I think. The proprietor was very displeased. We stay here at the end of every expedition. Always surprised me that Jumbo survived." Hagenbeck nodded towards the cloisters. "Filled with cages, not as many as I hoped. Two-thirds of the animals from Kassala always die, and we lost so many at sea. But here, what lives, we feed and water."

And made ready for the train, Nell was told. Jumbo and the other animals were packed into the boxcars so tightly, there was no chance of walking among the cages or pens, but the boxcars were open to night as the train swayed and clicked across dark fields glowing with lanterns of farmers caked with Nile. Jumbo had shared quarters with a giraffe, which could stand, but was no longer able. Scabs had formed over Jumbo's badly chewed feet, but at least he was not troubled by rats and struggled against his chains only once when a lamp in the next car fell, filling the train with the smoke of a soon-extinguished fire.

"We sailed that day to Trieste from Alexandria," concluded Hagenbeck, standing formally, leaving Nell running her fingers through blue lotuses in cool water under blue sky. "And tomorrow you and I sail to Suakin. Rest well. You will need it."

UNDER THE AWNING FLUTTERING OVER THE DECK AT THE STERN OF the *Mysore*, Nell applauded the boy, while dolphins leapt out of the frothy wake churning blue into green. She envied how cool the boy in the loincloth must feel, passenger or crew she never knew, and his lithe ability to dance while playing the lute.

"Smoke?" offered Hagenbeck, joining her.

He seemed to care not if women smoked, or maybe it was that a woman like Nell mattered not when it came to rules of propriety.

"We will have no secrets in the desert," he began frankly. "So I think you and Herr Scott, it is…love?" His statement was not meant to shock, merely observed.

Disarmed but not offended, Nell felt unexpectedly relieved at wanting to reply. "How can you know?"

"Eh, no woman crosses a desert for a man she hates. How long?"

"From the moment he saw who I am, not what I lack."

"Yes. I remember your Matthew Scott. An impenetrable man, but devoted."

To Jumbo.

White and crumbling structures clustered on the distant coast. "Suakin." Hagenbeck nodded. "From there, we cross the desert. Last chance to change your mind."

Nell's fingers enclosed the satin box in her pocket.

"Ottomans built the port, with elephants, so they say." Pirates scared off most of the trade, he explained, and the steamer paid to transport Hagenbeck and his animal captives, a quarter-century before. No knowing when another ship would slip past the pirates, and every day in Suakin, revenue died. With the unexpected arrival of the heavily laden *Zephyr* limping into port, Hagenbeck had bartered with the Turkish captain in the makeshift warehouse and taken inventory of his remaining menagerie.

Your animals, friend, said the Turkish man. So many! We have a full hold already.

They will fit?

Tightly so, very tight.

How long to Suez?

The captain gazed with intrigue at the juvenile elephant that would be Jumbo.

A week, if God is good, and we don't get boarded.

Over a meal of bread and olive oil and fish, passage was secured. The elephant calf was much admired.

You take it to Europe?

Yes, said Hagenbeck.

People pay to see it?

African ones are rare.

The *Zephyr*'s hold was hot and dark and airless, smoky from oil lamps. The men who worked down there wore bare strips of modesty and gasped for fresh air when they emerged. Chains were swung about Jumbo's neck and rang out as they were tightened and secured through an iron ring. Several men had to hold him, whimpering, as irons were secured about his feet, tethered so close to the rhino that they rubbed against each other.

With a partially full hold of copper ingots and wrapped bales of raw cotton, the other animals in cages were stacked so that the cats snarled and clawed relentlessly at the cowering hyenas below them. Birds fluttered and squawked in their dark confines while the giraffe was forced to kneel. Only the remaining ostrich entered this place with a quiet terror so often confused with dignity.

With the lamps extinguished and the hold secured, the animals battled wet heat to breathe. Jumbo groaned at the unfamiliar swaying and vomited as the *Zephyr* bobbed on the tide. When the steam engine hissed and rumbled, the noise and the ship pulling away from the dock rattled the animals and fired the hold with frightened screams.

Then came the rats, squeaking and scurrying, tickling Jumbo's feet as they swarmed around him and the rhino. But the rodents were hungry, and the tickling became nibbles, then bites. Jumbo railed but was too tightly chained to do little more than raise one foot a few inches, then another, and stomp at the biting rats. The floor beneath his feet became spongy and wet and crunchy, and still the rats came, until, exhausted, Jumbo leaned against the equally tormented rhino, and let the rats eat.

"But what could I do other than stick my head in and see what still breathed?" Hagenbeck was saying, the last ribbon of tobacco circling his bearded face. He tossed the remains into the sea. "Sailors would not go below."

The animals frightened them, the putrefying smell and furnace-like air made breathing impossible, and who'd notice anyway if the beasts were not fed and watered. Let the European stroll around up top and boast about how much money he'd make. Watering the animals, then, was nothing more than several buckets being splashed about; and as for feeding, eh, the animals could devour one another for all the crew cared.

"The rhino was dead, maybe a day before we noticed."

Quietly in the dark, slumping in irons, the weakly trumpeting Jumbo chained to his side.

"That night, off the coast of Safaga, we wrapped our faces against the stench, attached ropes to the bloated carcass, and dumped it overboard with the lion, almost all of the birds, and the ostrich."

CARAVAN TO KASSALA

Suakin, 1892

Suakin was a clogged warren of coral walls, shrouded women peering from cedar balconies, archways and cloisters where the scent from olive oil and turmeric hovered like a gnat-filled miasma, and where hibiscus, lush and tenacious, crowded doorways and trellises and rooftops with bouquets of orange and purple and peach.

Nell waited near the water trough, watching the German barter in the waterfront bazaar for men and animals to take them across the desert. They'd shed their European clothing for caftans and red plaid shemaghs. A group of children across the street called to her in Arabic, made faces, waved sticks, and threw rotten fruit, perhaps as enticement to play.

But closer inspection told the children something about the *boy* was not quite right, and they were tempted away by dust and stray dogs and a broken sack of pomegranates spilling into the street. In a place where diversions were rare and simple, how dazzling it must have been when Jumbo appeared: hardened, wind-burned men pulling, whipping, and pushing the remains of the German's pitiful and noisy menagerie through narrow streets, churning up the sandy road, leaving a trail of excrement and a mist of dust. Children running alongside camels, loaded with cages of birds and cats, the giraffe, ostriches, and the rhino being herded into the bazaar, covered from the sun, with open walls. How cooling the air from the Red Sea must have felt after days blistering under the sun. Cats tonguing at water trickled through bars. Water in barrels and hay for Jumbo and the rhino as the gathering curious pointed and giggled at the giraffe and ostriches, and distant through the arches, the gleaming white light tower across the water where small boats fished.

"We have men and camels." Hagenbeck strode towards her, shoving a pair of pistols into his belt.

"Do you need those?"

"When we leave Suakin, we'll need them."

Nell put out her hand. "Then give me one. I know how to shoot."

Hagenbeck hesitated, then thought the better of it. "*Meine Dame*, you do not stop amazing me."

RIDING A CAMEL ACROSS THE DESERT WAS A BIT LIKE RIDING JUMBO'S back under hot Hippodrome lights, without the cheering crowds. Without Scotty.

"It is too much for you?"

"I rode an elephant across the Brooklyn Bridge, Mr. Hagenbeck. You will do well to keep up with me."

But sandy winds she could do without.

The men of the caravan accepted her for the European's nephew, and if a closer look raised questions, they were paid enough not to care. Nell joined them around the fire for their common meals, understood nothing of their talk, and prayed nightly her throat wasn't slit while she slept. But Hagenbeck was at ease and promised her while eating the lamb stew that when they reached Kassala, he would take her to a woman famous for a dish of braised ibis that was said to have been Cleopatra's favourite.

Nothing like the steak served at Delmonico's; Nell vowed when she got home, she and Scotty would dine there. Maybe even invite Dora so she could hear what it was like to go weeks without a corset, and she may never wear one again.

"Bandits can see torches for miles out here in the dark." Hagenbeck was recounting that journey of his youth, flames from the fire darkening his thickening beard. "But we had no choice. Lose those animals in a week if we walked by day, men too."

Nell touched the pistol tucked under her caftan. Having choices felt comforting.

The German sounded almost wistful in his memories of that long-ago dawn, his first to collect animals, the vast and meandering caravan, bells and jingling harnesses, snapping whips, torches, and snarling, growling, mewling, thirsty, and hungry animals circling around Jumbo and the other elephant calf, a female, and the young rhino. Wagons piled with cats in iron cages: the lions, a cheetah, and several panthers. Water barrels, feed grass, and bread in crates fencing protectively on one side. Cages of monkeys, birds, madly pacing hyenas, and shivering civets hemming in larger animals on the other. Ostriches tethered to the camels so they would not wonder. Spilling across the sands beyond, scores of men with faces covered against the rising sun and sand, a few precious hours of peace from horses, camels, and goats chased by boys—*ya! ya! ya!*—and rowdy dogs. By full light, the herd was fed and watered and several of the goats gutted and bled before roasting. Bellies full, the men unfurled bedrolls and turned from the desert sun.

"But an infant covered more ground each day than we did, and we had hundreds of kilometres between Kassala and Suakin. And while young Jumbo took goat's milk, the female would not. Ah, the heartbreak of watching her value slip through my fingers."

Jumbo crossing Sudan was not the garrulous giant Hagenbeck recalled from that London Zoological Society dinner, but a gentle, frightened calf, caressing with another of his kind, making sounds much like crying. Jumbo fed grass into his mouth, his large, thickly lashed eyes timidly following the movements of men about the camp. The female sniffed at her feed but did not eat. Nearby, the baby rhino was already sleeping.

And slowly, each passing day, the struggling caravan unravelled across the desert. Water became scarce, animals hungered. The goats stopped giving milk. What died was cut up for the cats, raging after weeks crouching in their own filth. The men, bedding down to plaintive bellowing, slept brokenly, if at all.

"We sent riders along the northern trail to search for water, but the sun turned rivers into brick. Even the baobab deserted us. In dreams, I cut open their roots and drank from hidden seas."

Jumbo stumbled around carcasses littering the desert, following one of the ostriches, dragged in the sand by a camel until cut loose and left for the hovering carrion. The female elephant calf fell behind with birds left to die. One of the goatherds was ordered to prod her with a stick, but the slow-moving elephant angered the boy, who yelled and beat her through the night. In the morning, tied up by Jumbo and the rhino, she hung her head listlessly. Sometimes Jumbo caressed her face with his trunk, but she no longer cried.

When the calf collapsed, shouting boys and men tried to pull her back onto her feet, but she rolled over on her side, her big eyes blinking up at cloudless sky. Jumbo trumpeted weakly and rocked his head. Twenty leagues yet to the sea. She could not be carried.

"I wanted to shoot her," Hagenbeck concluded, "but why waste the bullet. We left her for the buzzards." Spoken so matter-of-factly, Nell concealed her disgust with the tasselled end of her shemagh so the German would not come to fear a woman with a pistol.

THE DOGS BROUGHT GREETINGS. BROWN DOGS. WHITE DOGS WITH curved tales and thin legs. Dogs with patchy colours, and spots, and thin fur. Barking and growling and yelping, circling indifferent, slow-moving camels, chased by barefoot children in dirty tunics, waving and greeting, some with sticks, at Nell and the others, escorting them through dust to the meandering market where open-air stalls shaded by cotton jingled with hanging clay pipes and lanterns, beaded necklaces and feathers, and twinkling, shimmering bits of silver adornments. Men jostling in narrow passages shouted prices with hand-clasped inducements for open sacks spilling with okra, celery seed, sorghum, coriander, cumin, and black pepper, and barrels of brownish-red cinnamon. Legs and loins and shanks of beef, sheep, and goats dried hanging under the sun. Birds awaited their fate in cages on bushels of onions, beneath gutted brethren hanging headless, while silent women whose keen eyes knew all and, as Nell wondered, may or may not have envied her ruse.

Hagenbeck noticed the delights of the market were lost on his companion. "You don't look well."

Ivory.

Towering piles swarming with gnats, ends black with dried blood. A graveyard of chess pieces, piano keys, cameos, and crucifixes.

"Ah, you have interest in the ivory market? The Aggageers sell their tusks here. They hunt the elephants. They took Jumbo."

Buyers came to bid in a dirt-packed square beyond the warren of the main market from as far as Khartoum, crowding three and four deep, others just to glimpse what could never be owned. White more valuable than gold.

"Men here still talk about the ivory from Jumbo's mother. Longer tusks have never been found."

This, after slow-moving weeks from the River Royan where Jumbo had been captured, his mother killed, along banks of dying rivers where he and the other captive animals could feed on thin grass and drink from muddy puddles before the hot season baked the land hard. Birds thrust into sacks hung in bundles, along with civets and monkeys, balking and bawling in wooden cages bouncing on the sides of camels. Giraffes and ostriches kept pace tethered to the backs of camels, while Jumbo and the young female and the rhino walked alongside, jabbed by boys with sticks. But slow meant the two elephant calves had survived at least to Kassala, as had the rhino, a miraculous feat. Those animals would fetch the biggest prices from the zoos in Paris and Berlin. Birds weren't so lucky. Those breaking their wings beating about in their sacks were left behind to flap about on the trail.

The first ivory buyer balked at the price demanded for a pile of tusks spread before him on woven mats, but his eyes betrayed his want. Such resplendent ivory, shaped and carved, would adorn the hair of only the richest women. Feel the most practised fingers of a virtuoso.

The loud and sometimes angry bartering could last for hours but, the German confided to Nell, men always agree on a price.

THE IVORY HUNTERS

East Sudan, 1892

"Look," pointed Hagenbeck, astride his camel beside Nell.

To where the savannah unrolled primordially to the horizon. Dotted by lonely, lofty acacia with wispy, shading canopies. Clusters of ever-moving gazelles and kudu and ibex grazed, ever wary of thick-necked hyenas prowling barely concealed in tall grass bleached and bent from the sun. A pride of lions lolled and frolicked and slept near the bloodied ribcage of a recent hunt, indifferent to sun-worshipping lizards sharing the castle-like outcrop of stone. A stork flapped, soared effortlessly. A muscular cheetah contemplated dinner. And there, far in the distance, elephants. Several younger grazing cows with their calves being led by a matriarch towards evening, a trailing lone bull watchful.

I feel him here. Scotty, I wish you could see this.

"I salute you, *meine Dame.* No Christian woman has been where you are."

This, after weeks sweltering under hot sun and ubiquitous sand, with foul-smelling camels and unwashed men who thought nothing of pissing in front of her or walking only a few steps to squat and shit, spitting and belching and breaking wind, often with a grin of missing or blackened teeth as if the effort worthy of a prize. Thankful for the small mercy of not understanding a word, although by the way Hagenbeck guffawed and manfully patted their backs, Nell dared not imagine. And always the worry that the mousy *nephew,* avoiding the gaze of men, would be uncovered. Not just a woman, but one like her. In this warrior world of trophies, what kind would she be?

THE TENTED AWNINGS OF THE AGGAGEERS' HUTS HUNG IN THE HOT air. Naked children stopped in mid-torment of a baby goat and wondered at the European's approach. Women were wrapped in layers of cotton but the men wore shiny bands of silver braided in their hair, and little else. Lithe and sinewy, muscles sliding just below skin glistening with sweat. Nell was staring and ought not to be.

"How far is the river?" she managed.

"A day, perhaps." Hagenbeck now bought his animals for the great zoos on the continent from the Aggageers in the markets of Kassala and so rarely came this far west. "But I was a young man then and it was my first trip to Africa. I wanted to see the hunt."

A good hunt already, he recalled. A baby elephant, the female. A young rhino. Giraffes. Ostriches. Unhappy doves, quails, and a flamingo in wooden cages. "But I was concerned about the calf. Two seasons old, the hunters told me. I thought she was too young and would not survive. I was right. I wanted another to be sure. Any zoo in Europe was willing to pay a fortune for an African elephant, and I was determined to bring at least one back."

But Jumbo's addition to the Aggageer camp was almost his undoing. One of the hunters had been mortally injured and the vengeful lamentations from his woman cut through the tented desert camp. Boys, cross and sharp with their retaliating sticks, herded Jumbo into a pen of woven branches where he limped to the centre to avoid the spitting children and their rain of stones.

Yo! Yo!

The elder, scattering the tormentors with waving arms unafraid to strike the slow-moving, wore a thick band of yellow wrapped around his head, stained from sweat about the brow. Unlike the nearly naked hunters, the keeper's tunic covered his body from the sun and was finely stitched with red symbols about the cuff. *Ah, ah,* he cooed gently, carrying a wooden bowl filled with water for Jumbo.

Why doesn't he drink? a much younger Hagenbeck asked, observing from outside the pen.

He will drink, the elder replied.

Will he die?

The keeper patted the small elephant calf on the back; he did not flinch, make a sound, or even raise his lowered head.

No, this one becomes large.

CAMELS WERE EXCHANGED FOR SURE-FOOTED HORSES STEPPING through bits of broken range littering the pass into the river valley where majestic baobabs soared above rolling savannah, vast, spreading canopies holding up bird and sky. Harnesses jingled. Broken rocks gave way to grass. By midday, the sun was high and hot.

"There." The German pointed to thick swathes of gamba.

Where an elephant slowly led her calf a quarter of a century before, where the river runs deep, where an elephant could still wade, and drink, and splash herself with cooling water. Others from her far-flung herd lumbered east during the night, and although this was her calf's second dry season and he could still run between her legs, grabbing her trunk playfully with his own, another sun or two, feasting on what remained of the dry reedy gamba, would strengthen him for their long march.

She pulled her calf towards her and let him slide his trunk into her mouth as she caressed the back of his head. Then the elephant filled her trunk, and with a short trumpet, sprayed her calf, her ears slowly beating away the hot dawn pooling about her face. The calf, first unsure as to the soft bottom, tossed water back, but mostly missed. Again and again, he snorted up the remains of the dark river as his mother lathered him with a cool spray and he continued even when play stopped and she raised her head at the scent of men.

Afraid, she waded quickly from the shallow river, cranes and grass parting for her, and called for her calf, who shook his head and bellowed rather than leave the cool water, the fun of tossing soft mud from the bottom over his back—a balm against the legion of flies and gnats. And because she would not leave him, the elephant saw the glint of silver too late, how men's skin glistened in morning, how their faces creased with a frenzied joy, how sure-footed horses flew over the embankments where the river etched through the valley, how sheaves of metal flashed when catching the sun.

She charged.

The men raced ahead of the elephant, circled back, crossed each other in front, infuriating her. The elephant roared. Another man, younger, shouting, his long hair coiled with silver bands, appeared hard at her flank, pulled ahead a few feet, and somersaulted from his horse. With his sword gripped tightly in his two hands, he swung, but the charging elephant seized him around the neck with her trunk. Cranes still gleaning the riverbank rose in noisy terror at the twisted wail when the elephant dragged him underfoot. The hunter's silence was abrupt.

Another took his place. Silver spun from his ears. Taller, thicker around the chest than the man who'd fallen, he rode more surely, gripped the leather reins more skillfully, but swung his sword overhead with a clear blind rage through tears. Closer and closer he pulled alongside the flank of the elephant, then pulled ahead of the charging animal, jumped down, knelt, and with both hands on his sword, swung through tendon and into bone. The elephant's front foot turned with a gush of red and the snapping of sinew. She crashed and tumbled in startled defeat to the dry, packed ground.

The hunter raced to the struggling and shrieking elephant and hacked above the foot of the other leg. She rolled her head towards him and stabbed with her tusks. With two arms raised, the hunter drove his sword into the elephant just behind the shoulder. His chest heaving, wiping sweat from his face with the back of his arm, he watched her heart pump wide red streams into the dirt.

They did not wait.

The weakening elephant railed against the men hacking with their swords at her white tusk, bone grinding and snapping, her head bouncing off the stone-like clay. She had no fight left when they ripped free the other ivory. Wiping the blood off his forearms, her killer rode back to the river. There, man and rope and horse pulled the calf free of the mud for the well-paying young German vomiting onto parched ground.

HOME, FREE

River Royan, 1892

The horizon brightened with orange. Hagenbeck and most of the other men in camp still slept, but the hungry and thirsty horses stirred and snorted. The man stoking the breakfast fire made no greeting as Nell passed on her way to the river.

She found it dying a slow and painful death, as it does once every full measure of seasons when dry northeasterlies from Arabia blow ancient sand across the Red Sea. Leaves drop from the towering baobabs. Jewelfish gasp in shallow puddles. The river becomes a thrashing scar under egrets poking noisily at its entrails. It was here that Nell sat, silent, the voices of men, now rising, back in the camp barely intruding. In her hands, the blue satin box for the man in her heart.

She watched and waited until, out of mist and morning and memory, they came. The elephant, slowly leading her calf, her magnificent ivory making way through squabbling shorebirds. They drank and ate from the gamba, played and forgave.

Follow us, Nell, but not yet.

She stood and tossed Jumbo's ivory back into the river.

He's home now, Scotty.

This time, no hunter would end their slow march to Abyssinia.

MUMBO JUMBO

Medford, 1893

Even with fur wrapped about her knees, Nell shivered as the carriage cut through icy streets, her breath expelled as white mist. Already broken was her vow to never again complain about the cold. In her haste, she'd left her trunks at the station. No matter, they'd soon be on their way somewhere. Anywhere. But she was happy in the not knowing. Every day was a promise now, her dream, and while this sad chapter was coming to an end, it offered a beginning of sorts.

Long weeks back to Alexandria, empty hours adrift on the Mediterranean, storm-tossed passage from London, imagining the look on Scotty's face the moment she told him she'd made it to the river. Jumbo was home. Scotty taking comfort, as best could be. He had to, just had to. Maybe find peace in a goodbye. Maybe start a dream, their dream, as she dared to hope. No more Mr. Scott. Her own, dear Scotty. If only the windows were not frosted, Nell could see how much farther.

Without warning, the driver barked to the horse, the carriage slowed and stopped. The door opened, the outside air stung. Nell hurried up steps to the tall, thin boarding house. The knocker too high, she rapped with hands until a girl answered, flustered. Her hair was wrapped in a kerchief printed with pineapples. She curtsied, as if remembering an instruction.

"I've come to see Mr. Scott." Nell brushed past the girl, pulling off her gloves, hand reaching for the banister.

"Oh, ma'am." Something in the way the girl spoke and how she glanced to the top of the stairs. "That gentleman's not here."

Of course, he was. The girl must be newly employed. Where else would he be? And damn that Hamburg dressmaker for talking her into tighter stays. Nell could barely breathe, but she vainly wanted to show off her figure to its best advantage. She was gasping by the top of the landing, the door slightly ajar, creaking when it pushed open, the room empty and cold, hearth scrubbed and bare. The bed's mattress gone, so too the small table and wicker chair by the window.

Laboured steps followed her.

"Ah, look what the cat's dragged in." Mrs. Meck rubbed her hands in an apron washed thin.

"Where is he?"

"Fine time I had with your Mr. Scott, I can tell you that, madam. Drink, you said to me. Nothing about him being mad as a lunatic. *Jumbo. Jumbo. Jumbo.* Screaming that name at all hours of the night."

Nell wanted to ask if he'd shouted any other names, but she knew Scotty hadn't.

"No bother when he wasn't drinking, and count the days on one hand for that, but a right sorrowful demon when he did. Knocking about up here, back and forth, keeping us awake all hours. Oh, don't you be looking at me like I held the good Lord's hand when the nail went in. Men always find a way back to the devil, all on their own. And when he got so's none of us could handle him, I don't mind saying, I gave him a cup or two myself."

"What? Are you evil, or just dull-witted?" Instructions were given, instructions to be followed. Drink to a drunk! That doe-eyed girl downstairs looked to have more sense than this foolish woman.

"I'll not have that tone from you, lady. No word for months. Money gone. Had to get my lad, Martin, to sit with him, worried I was, letting the place burn down over us. How'd I know you'd come back and settle accounts? You could've been off God knows where, with a new fella. Women do that when they find their man's only fit for the bottle. And I know sure as peas in a pod, when fellas get this bad, drink's the only medicine that works. At least it quiets them down."

Nell looked beyond the window, the fingertip of her white glove blackening as she pulled it down the glass. Her taffeta dress rustled under Mrs. Meck's disapproval, or possibly, envy.

"What happened to him?"

"What that man got up to after he left is his own affair."

Nell swung back, incredulous at the woman's callousness. "How could you let him go?"

"I run a boarding house, madam, not a prison. Your Mr. Scott got out one night, bad night as he ever had. Sat right in front of that door long as I could, keeping my other lodgers from tossing him out the window—out of courtesy to you. And only for the salvation of my own soul, not expecting payment, mind you. Townsfolk found him out there." Mrs. Meck nodded to the snow-blown fields surrounding Tufts College.

Jumbo.

Nell understood why when she realized the woman was still talking.

"...took him to a charity house—"

"He's alive?"

"Didn't hear nothin' to the contrary."

"Where?"

"Boston, I expect. Church folk there always trying to save them lost souls. Body too far gone if you ask—"

Nell was through the door and halfway down the stairs.

"Now you wait right there, madam. Madam? What about my bill?" Mrs. Meck followed Nell down, but she was large and the stairs narrow and the bannister wiggled and she had to step sideways. "I'm owed, madam! That fellow caused me no end of grief and I'll not be cheated by the likes of you!"

The girl with the pineapple kerchief waited at the bottom, holding open the door. She looked to enjoy slamming it shut just after Nell stepped out onto the porch and into the waiting carriage.

AT THE END OF A LONG HALLWAY, MRS. JOYFUL CANTON RESTED formidably behind her desk as if she were buttressing the feet of God against all manner of sin and annoyance. Behind her, multi-coloured apostles framed a square of window overlooking a frozen garden. Her white blouse was simple, covering her wrists to the top of her neck, adorned with a heavy gold cross. The plain skirt allowed for purposeful movement through the almshouse wards, where she oversaw the dispatching of men fallen from grace, as quickly as possible, without further strain to the public purse. Mrs. Canton was, however, not without compassion, and she ensured the diseased and convulsing expired on clean sheets, a final ration, and as many Bible verses as could be tolerated in the hours remaining. As an unshakable believer in the sins of the father being visited upon the child, she could only imagine what great evil had been committed by Nell's parents.

"I used to be P. T. Barnum's biggest attraction," she began, smiling tightly. "Best to get that out of the way. Don't you agree?"

Mrs. Canton realized she'd been staring and tried not to, but Nell's dress was yellow and blood orange, colours best described as glorious but sinful. Her hair was a hue of red, but not the red of a respectable woman. And small. So tiny in fact, even though her back did not touch the chair, her feet dangled in front of her like a child. She might easily have passed for one if not for the lines about her eyes and mouth and the professional yet unsuccessful attempt to conceal them.

"I'm looking for a man. Matthew Scott."

"You are family?"

"No."

"I thought not. You have reason to believe he's here?"

"He was last seen in Medford."

Mrs. Canton pulled over a well-thumbed leather-bound ledger and opened the pages. Her finger traced mechanically down columns.

"No Matthew Scott recorded, but often men are too ashamed to give a name. They'd rather die alone than see the tears they've caused on the face of a loved one. Have you tried the other almshouses?"

"You're my last hope. Could he have been discharged?"

"We are the last stop on the road to Jesus."

Nell, ever hopeful, recalled Scotty the last time she saw him. His manner, height, weight—the intensity of his gaze, rough but gentle hands, the smell of tobacco like perfume—didn't think about the whiskey, dreadfully thin, racking cough. But surely redeemable.

"And English. He's English."

"An Englishman..." Mrs. Canton's finger was back on a column. "I recall that one. Near frozen to death when they brought him in. Methodists, I believe. The doctor noted here delirium tremens. Troublesome man. We never knew his name. Disturbed the others, you understand. Going on about too much room. One can never make sense of these wretched souls when the end nears, and your Mr. Scott was in a hurry to go. A great sin, if you ask me. Refused to stay quietly in the wards. We had to move him."

"Yes? Where?"

"We put him in the stables. Until the end."

Like an animal. Of all eventualities—not this. "Alone?"

Mrs. Canton, without apology, folded her hands in judgment.

Ah, yes. Faith. *Leap off this mountain, fall endlessly through cloud and hope to pass through the eye of a needle.* Nell fumbled for a handkerchief, then demanded better of herself. Scotty didn't die here; he'd followed Jumbo long ago to a river under desert stars. She'd been foolishly running to catch up ever since. In weeks, that square of window would be open to a spring Scotty wouldn't see. Such a beautiful waste. But his last words that night, they were for now.

Save yourself.

"Did...he ask for anyone?"

"Nothing but mumbo jumbo."

"Was he buried?" asked Nell, bluntly.

"We had no family, no friend to advise—"

"Where?"

"Potters Field."

Nell slid from the chair, her shoes clicking on the floor, took as deep a breath as her corset allowed. But she was not to be pitied.

"Will you be all right?" Mrs. Canton, standing, asked by rote.

You mean, someone like me?

She'd walked across water in the shadow of giants. Raced camels over the sands of Africa. New York and London had shouted her name. And yes, someone like her had managed to find a kind of love. Mrs. Joyful Canton, and the world, would not see a single tear. And while it seemed impossible to her now, all Nell had to do was walk back through the long hallway and into what remained.

A vintage engraving of children taking a ride on the back of Jumbo, The London Illustrated News, *1882.*

AFTERWORD

While *Jumbo* is a work of fiction, Jumbo the African elephant—*Loxodonta africana*—was not. Thought to have been born in 1860 and taken from the wilds between Sudan and present-day Eritrea in 1862 (where, it should be noted, elephants have been hunted to near extinction), Jumbo was sold to the Jardin des Plantes in Paris, from where he was subsequently purchased by the London Zoological Gardens in 1865. Jumbo remained in London until sold by Superintendent Abraham Bartlett, as much to rid the zoo of the potential dangers of an unpredictable elephant entering musth as the animal's taciturn keeper who'd become a law unto himself. Although feared for being belligerent and destructive, thousands nonetheless paid to sit on Jumbo's howdah for a ride around the zoo—including Queen Victoria's children, Prince Leopold and Princess Beatrice, and a young lad who would later become prime minister, Winston Churchill—earning Jumbo the nickname "The Children's Friend."

Fame when it came, was unrelenting.

In our age of global celebrity, *likes*, and viral sensations, it may be surprising to learn just how famous Jumbo really was in the nineteenth century. After his sale to P. T. Barnum, Jumbomania swept England, embroiled the Houses of Parliament, erupted into open warfare in the British and American press, and monopolized popular kitsch and culture. When Jumbo sailed into New York on the *Assyrian Monarch*, he was no less of a sensation, mostly due, perhaps, to Barnum's marketing acumen. Thousands clamoured for a glimpse, not only in New York, but across the northeastern United States and southern Canada. Jumbo did in fact, lead an elephant walk across the newly built Brooklyn Bridge on May 17, 1884, to convince residents of its safety. And when he was tragically killed by a train in St. Thomas Ontario, in 1885, the *New York Times* lamented: "The Great Jumbo Killed." Before Barnum died in 1891, he gifted Tufts College, now Tufts University, with Jumbo's mounted hide, where it held court in the atrium of Barnum Hall until destroyed by fire in 1975. His bones are in the American Museum of Natural History in New York.

What little we know about Matthew Scott comes from a thin and fanciful autobiography he completed months before Jumbo's death. Born in 1834 on the Knowsley estate of Lord Derby in Lancashire, he was one of seventeen children. At first attending to the parrots in the Earl's private menagerie, he eventually excelled in the caring of prized South African elands. In 1851, after the earl died and left his elands to the London Zoological Society, it was arranged for Scott to settle them in their new home. He never returned to Knowsley. In addition to the elands, Scott was recognized for caring for the cassowaries and an apteryx. A quiet, hard-working man, when the zoo purchased Jumbo in 1865, it was Scott the superintendent sent to Paris to retrieve him. By all accounts, for the rest of Jumbo's life, Matthew Scott never left his side. No record has been found of Scott's death or burial.

While this is a work of fiction, I believed it important to stay within the framework of the facts. Where I've strayed, *mea culpa*. Fiction is a demanding taskmaster. To the following who went before me and lived it, or did the heavy lifting, I am indebted:

Autobiography of Matthew Scott, Matthew Scott, Trow's Printing and Bookbinding Co., Bridgeport, 1885.

Jumbo, W. P. Jolly, Constable and Company Ltd, London, 1976.

"Jumbo, The Life of an Elephant Superstar," *The Nature of Things with David Suzuki,* season 57, Episode 10.

Jumbo, The Unauthorised Biography of a Victorian Sensation, John Sutherland, Aurum Press Ltd, London, 2014.

Jumbo, This Being the True Story of the Greatest Elephant in the World, Paul Chambers, Steerforth Press, Hanover, 2008.

London Zoo from Old Photographs 1852–1914, John Edwards, Butler Tanner and Dennis, 2012.

P. T. Barnum, The Legend and the Man, A. H. Saxon, Columbia University Press, New York, 1989.

Selected Letters of P. T. Barnum, A. H. Saxon, ed., Columbia University Press, New York, 1983.

"The Great Jumbo Killed," *The New York Times,* September 17, 1885.

Wild Animals in Captivity Being an Account of the Habits, Food, Management and Treatment, of the Beasts and Birds at the Zoo, A. D. Bartlett, Chapman and Hall Ltd, London, 1899.

AND WHILE LITTLE NELL KELLY IS, OF COURSE, A FICTIONAL character, there's no reason not to imagine something of her fate:

Finding circus life constraining after riding a camel across Sudan, Nell found work in what would become vaudeville, gradually finding her way to silent films where, in 1912 at the age of forty-nine, she became a stunt double for, and great friend to, Mary Pickford. For her efforts selling war bonds—*Fund the Guns, Beat the Huns!*—and entertaining her Canadian countrymen at the front during the First World War, George V made her a Dame of the British Empire. She lived for many years in a seaside cottage in Bournemouth, dying peacefully at the age of eighty-four, never again speaking of Jumbo.

Or Matthew.

She is buried at Highgate in London under a bronze tablet inscribed with her name: *Mercy Augustine Eccleston.*

NICOLA DAVISON

Stephens Gerard Malone has been lured by his protagonists for years, from rural Musquodoboit Harbour to the storied shores of the Bedford Basin, the Sachsenhausen concentration camp outside Berlin to the legendary London Zoo. A settler grateful to be writing in unceded Mi'kma'ki, the author of *Big Town* and *The History of Rain*, *Jumbo* is his sixth novel.